Fourth-Grade
Weirdo

FOURTH-GRADE WEIRDO

Martha Freeman

A YEARLING BOOK

35 Years of Exceptional Reading

Yearling Books
Established 1966

Published by
Dell Yearling
an imprint of
Random House Children's Books
a division of Random House, Inc.
1540 Broadway
New York, New York 10036

Visit us on the Web! www.randomhouse.com/kids

**Educators and librarians, for a variety of teaching tools,
visit us at www.randomhouse.com/teachers**

ISBN: 0-440-41689-2

Reprinted by arrangement with Holiday House, Inc.

Printed in the United States of America

August 2001

10 9 8 7 6 5 4 3 2 1

OPM

For my cousin Al Hupp
who has never been a weirdo
but does like a well-ordered life.

Fourth-Grade Weirdo

Chapter One

Mr. Ditzwinkle is standing on his hands again. The cuffs of his pants flop down to his knees, and everybody can see his hairy legs. Some keys, two pens and a purple marble drop out of his pockets and *clatta-clink* to the floor. In a minute his glasses will fall off. When he's back on his feet, he'll step on them.

It's not even Halloween, and already it takes practically an entire roll of masking tape to hold Mr. Ditzwinkle's glasses together. What will they look like in June?

Anyway, standing on his hands works. Except for a couple of giggles at the hairy legs, the class gets quiet.

I roll my eyes. All right already, Mr. Ditz. You can come down now.

"Ta-da!" He jumps to his feet. Tiffany T-1, major kiss-up of the universe, claps like we're watching a circus star, not just our show-off fourth-grade teacher. A couple other kiss-up girls join her.

When Mr. Ditzwinkle is right side up, he has curly black hair that droops over his forehead. He wears lotsa-color shirts that have flowers or bugs or stripes on them. Even though he is not that old for a grown-up, he is getting fat around the middle. I think he should so some sit-ups. I do twenty-five before bed every night.

"No applause, plea—" Mr. Ditzwinkle starts to say, but—*crrr-r-r-a-a-ck*—he's interrupted. What did I tell you? There went the glasses.

Mr. Ditzwinkle makes a face and scoops them off the floor, along with the junk from his pockets. "Okay, guys!" he says. "Let's get down with some education!" Then he starts telling us the art assignment, and all the time he talks he feels around on the desk behind him, searching for the tape.

". . . a self-portrait. Use whatever medium you like—pencil, watercolor, glitter, even torn paper. Just be sure to be creative!"

The room erupts with kids going for the art supplies. Mr. Ditzwinkle is opening the drawers in his desk, one after the other, still looking for tape. I raise my hand.

"Yes, Dexter?"

"Could I maybe do some arithmetic extra credit instead?" I ask.

"Aha!" Mr. Ditzwinkle holds up the masking tape like it's a trophy. Then he rips off a piece and wraps it round and round and round his broken glasses. "You're way ahead in math now, Dexter. Don't you want to express your creative side?"

"How about spelling?" I try. "I'm not so far ahead in spelling."

"Self-portrait," Mr. Ditzwinkle says firmly. "Close your eyes. Think about the handsome guy you are inside. Then get the glue! The glitter! The paint! Express the you-ness of you!"

The you-ness of you? I shake my head. Whatever channel Mr. Ditz is tuned to, it's coming from way, way out there.

At the desk on my right, Josh Golden is drawing a yellow half circle in the top corner of a big sheet of paper. It's a sun. He fills it in neatly. Then he draws a row of short lines with the same yellow crayon. Hair.

"Do you want to borrow my ruler?" I whisper. "To make your hairs straighter?"

"Aw, that's okay, Dex. I never comb my hair anyway."

That's obvious, I think. But I would never say that. Josh is the nicest guy in the universe. He looks good even with mussed-up hair.

In front of me, Tiffany T-2 is gluing red sequins on a sheet of pink paper. She squeezes a drop of glue on the paper, traps a sequin on the tip of her finger, presses the sequin down on the glue. One. She squeezes another drop of glue, traps a sequin, presses the sequin. Two. Whatever she's making, it will take for-crying-out-loud-ever.

She sees me watching and says, "It's a heart."

"You're not doing the assignment right. It's supposed to be you," I answer.

"It's the *real* me," she says. Then she tosses her hair and blinks four times fast at Josh. Lucky for him, he's not paying attention. "The real me is *brimming* with love." Blink-blink-blink-blink.

Tiffany T-2 is really Tiffany Tremayne. Tiffany T-1 is really Tiffany Tasso. Any other teacher in the entire universe who got stuck with two Tiffany T's in the same class would use their full names. Not Mr. Ditzwinkle.

Uh-oh, here he comes. He's going up and down the rows to see how everybody's doing. In a second, he'll see I'm not doing at all. He won't like it if I tell him the best way to express the me-ness of me is in a multiplication problem.

I don't have any choice, so I get paper, a pencil and a ruler out of my briefcase. Let's see. Six inches looks good. What else? Oh yeah. Eyes.

Mr. Ditzwinkle pauses at each desk and says, "Nice job," or "Terrific!"

Now he's looking over my shoulder. He doesn't say anything, but I can hear him breathing. My stomach starts worrying. Maybe I'll have to start over. Finally he says, "Well, Dexter . . . very, uh . . . symmetrical." Then he moves on to Josh.

Symmetrical? Is that good?

I wish I understood Mr. Ditzwinkle. Last year when I had Mrs. Dinsmore, things were easy. I was quiet. I raised my hand. I wrote neatly. Mrs. Dinsmore thought I was perfect.

But with Mr. Ditz, all the rules are different—or maybe there aren't any rules at all.

Chapter Two

Today we do arithmetic after lunch. Every fourth-grade class in the universe has a schedule, right? Except us. Sometimes we do arithmetic in the morning. Sometimes we do it right before recess. Sometimes we don't do it at all. Mr. Ditzwinkle calls this "spontaneous." I call it crazy.

The class is getting rowdy again. After Mr. Ditz said "arithmetic," there was a big moan and grumble, like he was announcing we all needed tetanus shots. Only Tommy Finch and I have our calculators ready.

Tommy Finch, smartest kid in the universe, sits in the front row. When he talks he always sounds like NPR, the radio station my parents listen to. Never an *um* or a *like* or a *you know* like a normal kid. It's spooky.

That's not the worst thing about Tommy Finch, either. The worst is he knows everything. Not *thinks* he knows everything. Really *does* know everything. There's a rumor that his dad is a super-brain who lives in a white tower at the university and communicates only by computer.

So of course nobody in the whole entire fourth grade at Prospect Avenue Elementary likes Tommy Finch. Except for probably Josh. Because Josh likes everybody. Even me.

A paper airplane just nose-dived into the wastebasket. Two points. In about a minute, somebody will get hit with a spit wad. But wait! Mr. Ditzwinkle makes his eyebrows go halfway up his head. Right away people shush each other. When Mr. Ditz's eyebrows crawl around like caterpillars, we know something strange is about to happen.

Everybody's watching as Mr. Ditzwinkle picks up two long pieces of white chalk and holds them in front of his face.

"An arithmetic problem," he says. "If we have two pieces of chalk, and we subtract two pieces of chalk, how many remain?"

All the class geniuses yell, "Zero!" Before they even get the second syllable said, Mr. Ditz snaps his fingers and the chalk disappears.

"Oh, Mr. Ditzwinkle, that was *wonderful!*" Tiffany T-1 gushes.

"How'd he do that?" Josh whispers to Tommy Finch.

"Sleight of hand," Tommy Finch answers. "While the audience is distracted by—"

"Okay, guys!" Mr. Ditzwinkle says so loudly that nobody can hear Tommy Finch. "Let's get down with some education! Today we've got something special for math." He reaches under his desk and pulls out a giant jar filled with jelly beans.

What do jelly beans have to do with math? Can't we for once just do problems from worksheets?

Mr. Ditz explains that we are going to work in teams and make a bar graph. The graph will show how many jelly beans of each kind are in the jar. "After math, we'll have the jelly-bean race," he goes on. "We set the stopwatch and see how fast you can eat a whole lot of jelly beans."

It takes a second for that to sink in. Then Eric, problem child of the universe, bounces up and hollers a big *"Yesssss!"* Now the whole class is asking, "Can we eat 'em? Can we? Huh? Huh? Huh?"

Everybody but me and Tommy Finch has forgotten all about arithmetic.

Two minutes later the teams are forming, and Josh tells Amber that I eat only black jelly beans. Thanks a lot, Josh. I'm already the official second-weirdest kid in fourth grade. If it turns out Tommy Finch likes lotsa-color jelly beans, I'll move right into the Number 1 spot.

But instead I'm all of a sudden everybody's pal.

"*Please*, Dex—be on our team," begs Amber, who has bouncy curls and always looks perfect. Her mom's on TV.

"No! Dexter, I swear. If you're on our team, I'll never say another word about your dweebacious briefcase. Honest, no kidding, and truly-for-sure." That's Paula, my mortal enemy.

It takes a couple seconds before I figure out everybody wants my lotsa-color jelly beans. Most of the time, the IQs of my Room 29 classmates are not sky high. But when it comes to dividing jelly beans or marshmallows or cupcakes, everybody's a genius.

I let everybody beg me a little longer, then I pick Josh's team. After all, he's my friend even without jelly beans. Also on the team is Marlee Ann, and then—*oh no*—Mr. Ditzwinkle tells us we have to take Eric.

Like I said, Eric is the problem child of the universe. And his mom is even worse. The thing about his mom is, she's running for school board against my mom, and she goes all over town saying mean things. Of course, I know Eric's mother is not Eric's fault, and it's not fair to hate him. But there's so much to hate him for.

Anyway, right now Eric is bouncing in the seat like he has to go to the bathroom bad. Only he doesn't. He just always bounces.

Mr. Ditzwinkle pours a bag of jelly beans out of the jar for each team. Marlee Ann has the best handwriting, so she draws our graphs. Josh is the nicest, so he divides up the jelly beans. My job is to do the math, of course. Eric doesn't have to do anything except try not to wreck it all. For Eric, that's enough of a job.

I count up the reds, thirteen. But when I double-check, I get eleven.

The rest of us look hard at Eric.

He tries to smile all innocent, but there's red slobber on his front teeth.

Marlee Ann looks terrified. She is the type that would rather die than get in trouble. She probably thinks they'll send us back to third grade if we muff this jelly-bean graph. "What *now*?" she asks.

"Use thirteen," Josh says, "and if Eric eats any more before we're done, we brain him." That's how annoying Eric is. He even drives Josh crazy.

Marlee's making the last bar when Mr. Ditzwinkle comes over. He tells her the graph looks good. You can see she's relieved he didn't figure out about Eric's subtraction problem. Then he notices my jelly beans and asks how come I got stuck with black ones.

"They're the only ones I like," I say.

Mr. Ditz shakes his head. "I never heard of a kid who likes only black jelly beans."

It's then that he gives me the frown. It's only a flash. I probably wasn't even supposed to see it. But I did see it, and here's what it said: "I don't like you, Dexter Plum."

I feel the way Tommy Finch must when the kickball mows him down. I don't like Mr. Ditzwinkle, but I didn't think it worked the other way. I thought teachers *had* to like the kids in their class. I thought it was in their contract. And contracts are something I know about. My dad's a lawyer.

"Whatsamatter, Dex?" Josh is staring at me. "You look sick."

I don't know what to say. I just shake my head and watch Mr. Ditzwinkle walk over to Tommy Finch's group. Sure enough, Tommy

Finch is chewing on a handful of lotsa-color jelly beans.

So that clinches it. Dexter Plum, who likes only black jelly beans, whose very own teacher hates him, is officially the fourth-grade weirdo.

CHAPTER THREE

Every kid at Prospect Avenue Elementary knows the final bell beeps at 3:15 and 21 seconds. It's now 3:14, jelly beans are bubbling in our bellies, and Mr. Ditzwinkle is reading us a story about turbo-charged grandmas. It's a good story, but I can't wait to get out of here.

When the second hand on the clock lurches to 3:15, I count off the seconds. One . . . two . . . three . . . You have to go slow, which is tough when you're aching for freedom. Eight . . . nine . . . ten . . . Who's that yelling in the corridor? Thirteen . . . fourteen . . . fifteen . . .

Six seconds before the beep, this big purple grown-up gusts into our room. Right behind her is a smaller, skinnier grown-up: Ms. Morf, the office secretary. Mr. Broomhockey is our principal, but the Morf runs the school. Usually nobody messes with her. "I cannot permit this disruption!" she says in this careful way she has. "You must observe procedures! Please return to—"

The bell beeps, but nobody moves. We want to see what happens next.

"Well, I *am* sorry, but school's over, isn't it?" says the purple person. "And I do have a campaign appearance to get to. Now . . ." She turns and I see it's Eric's mom, Mrs. Gale, my mom's archenemy.

Mrs. Gale does not actually have purple skin. She's just wearing a purple hat and a long purple coat. She ignores the Morf, who is still arguing.

"I want that PC money," she huffs at Mr. Ditzwinkle. "Yours is the *last* class to turn in its envelope. Mrs. *Dinsmore's* class had one *hundred* percent participation!"

Mr. Ditzwinkle tilts his head so his busted glasses slide across his nose. "PC money?" he repeats. "Who are you anyway?"

"Oh, for *heaven's* sake. My face is on signs all over the neighborhood!"

"O-o-o-oh. Then you're a dangerous criminal?" Mr. Ditzwinkle tries to sound innocent, but he can't help it—he busts up laughing. The Morf laughs, too. That might be a first.

"Very funny," Mrs. Gale says. "I'm Sheila Gale, candidate for school board. You surely know my slogan: 'Well-formed minds in uniformed bodies'?" Mrs. Gale puts her hand out. She must go door-to-door like my mom does. You say your name, you shake hands. It's automatic.

Mr. Ditzwinkle takes her hand and lifts it toward his face like—oh, *gross!*—he's going to kiss it or something. Mrs. Gale looks terrified, and there's the beginning of an "e-e-e-e-wwwww!" from the boys. Just in time, Mr. Ditz lets go. "Charmed, I'm sure," he says. "As for you"— he looks at the class—"it's *adios* and *hasta la pasta, amigos.*"

There's a big moan and grumble, but everybody zips their backpacks, and I buckle my briefcase.

I'm half out the door when Mr. Ditzwinkle says, "Dexter? Can you hang out a moment, please? I'll be right with you."

Now what? Right away my stomach starts to worry.

Meanwhile, Eric is trying to sneak past his mom. But she catches sight of him, and he's trapped. "You're not going anywhere, squirt," she tells him. "I need you in case the newspaper sends a photographer this afternoon. Remember?"

Eric looks like a swatted fly.

When the other kids are gone, Mr. Ditzwinkle says to Eric's mom, "Now, just what are you talking about? What is this PC thing anyway?"

"Oh, for *heaven's* sake!" Mrs. Gale huffs. "The PC is the Parents Club! I'm the treasurer this year, and I *need* the membership money."

"Oh, that," says Mr. Ditz. "I have it here somewhere. About two hundred dollars? I'll give it to Ms. Morf tomorrow. Okie doke?"

"No, it is *not* 'okie doke.'" Mrs. Gale looks at her watch. "I'm giving a speech in seventeen minutes. I expect you to find that money *now*!"

Mr. Ditzwinkle shrugs, reaches into his pants pocket and pulls out a fortune cookie fortune, a bubble-gum wrapper, a plastic glow-in-the-dark salamander and—hey!—two long pieces of white chalk. "Not here," he says. "Sorry. I'll give it to Ms. Morf tomorrow. Now, if you'll excuse me, I have to talk to Dexter or he'll miss his bus."

In fact, I don't ride the bus. But this is not the time to mention it.

Mrs. Gale opens her mouth and closes it. Then she looks from Mr. Ditzwinkle to the Morf to me and down to Eric. Finally she lets go with this huge *harrumph*, turns her back and strides out.

Eric gives us a look that says, "Don't blame me; I didn't pick her," then he runs after her. The Morf follows them both down the corridor. I think she wants to make sure Her Purpleness really leaves.

As soon as they're good and gone, Mr. Ditzwinkle says, "I want you to help me hang the self-portraits, Dexter." Then he puts on the raggedy orange jacket he wears to school every day. Its pockets sag, they are so loaded down with junk. He should get a briefcase, like me.

He grabs a handful of thumbtacks from a jar on his desk, and I follow him into the corridor. That's where our class hangs all the art projects. He gives me the thumbtacks, which prickle my palms.

"What do you think of these?" Mr. Ditz asks.

He puts up Amber's portrait. It has yellow curly ribbons for hair and a white blouse made out of an old piece of lace. It looks perfect, just like Amber. Then he puts up Marlee Ann's, which has button eyes and a dress cut out of polka-dot cloth.

I shrug. "Good."

I hand him another tack, and he sticks it in Zeke's. For a nose, Zeke folded a strip of green paper accordion-style and stuck two black nostril dots on the end. This makes his portrait look like a sort of cross between an elephant and a space alien. I guess that's the Zeke-ness of Zeke.

Next comes mine. Mr. Ditzwinkle looks down at it, then up at me, then down at it and up at me again.

I scratch my head, look at the gray linoleum floor squares, shuffle my feet. I wish Mr. Ditzwinkle would for-crying-out-loud put my picture on the wall so I can go home. Finally he says, "Perhaps you'd like to paint it?"

"I'm not that colorful."

"Or add something? You can make great-looking eyebrows with staples."

I shake my head. What does he want from me? My picture's okay. Not as fancy as the other ones, but okay. "That's who I am," I say.

"Dexter." Mr. Ditz is exasperated, I can tell. "I don't think this is the real you, is it? The handsome guy inside?"

How am I supposed to know the real me? I'm nine years old and I carry a briefcase. What else is there to know?

Now we're both looking at my self-portrait. It's a six-inch square face I made with my ruler, two quarter-size eyes I made with my compass, and a big frowning 180-degree curve I made with my protractor. I drew it in pencil, then went over it with black marker.

"Dexter," he tries again, "are you unhappy?"

If I was, I wouldn't tell *you,* I think. But you can't say that to your teacher.

Mr. Ditzwinkle sighs. "Okay, okay. Just one more thing. A long time ago there was an old guy by the name of Polonius. He talked funny 'cause it was long ago, right? Anyway, he gave a kid the same piece of advice I'm going to give you, and this is it: To thine own self be true."

An old guy named Polonius? Phooey. What's the Ditz talking about now?

Walking home, I make a list of people who like me. My mom and dad. My three grandparents. Josh Golden. I come up with those six the first block.

For once, I wish I had a brother or a sister. That might be somebody else that would like me. But Mom and Dad always say I'm so great, why would they want to take a chance on another kid?

Now I'm passing the stores downtown, still thinking. The thrift store has winter coats in the window, two dollars each. I notice new baseball mitts at All Sortsa Sports. And model dinosaurs at Hobby Lobby. The dinosaurs make me remember third grade when we studied them. And that makes me think of Mrs. Dinsmore. She likes me. That's seven.

I turn the corner at Gentleman's Closet. There are black bomber jackets in the window. SALE! says the sign, $199.95! Dad likes those kind of jackets. But $199.95 would be my allowance for—I do the math—forty weeks, with a nickel left over.

When I get to the streets with houses, I count the campaign signs in the yards. Three for mom and two for Mrs. Gale—just like yesterday. On our block, there are two more for my mom. Josh Golden's house next door, and ours of course.

As I walk by Josh's, I wonder how many people like Mr. Ditzwinkle. Everybody likes him. No, everybody *loves* him. Everybody except me.

Chapter Four

Every day after school, Mom gives me the same snack:

- four gingersnaps
- a carrot's worth of carrot sticks
- one glass of milk

It's the best snack in the universe. I'm going to be a lawyer like my dad, and I plan to eat it every day after college, every day after law school, and every day after court.

I like to plan things like that out. Life is crazy enough. Who wants surprises?

Today Mom puts my snack on the kitchen counter, sits down and asks for the report.

"Three for you, two for Mrs. Gale—not counting us and the Goldens," I say.

Then she wants to know how come I'm late. I tell her I had to help after school. I don't tell her I figured out Mr. Ditz doesn't like me. I already know what she'd say: "Oh, Dexter, I'm sure you're imagining things. Why wouldn't he like a perfect student like you?"

Then I tell her how her archenemy Mrs. Gale came into our class and Mr. Ditz couldn't find the PC money.

Mom laughs, which is not what I expected. I think Mrs. Gale is scary.

"I would vote for you instead of her anytime," I say, "except—I dunno—maybe it would be cool to wear a uniform to school. Like Dad's army uniform."

Mom punches her chest and drops her head like she's been stabbed. "Cut me to the quick!" she says. "No kid of mine is wearing a uniform to a public school."

"I only meant—" I begin, but she's not paying attention.

"It's un-American, an abridgment of children's rights." She stands up. "You know, Dexter, it's a matter of free speech, what our forefathers fought and died for. Valley Forge . . . Gettysburg . . . Iwo Jima!" Her voice echoes around the house. "Remember the *Maine*!"

"Mom," I say, "you don't have to convince *me*. I'm your *kid*. And besides, the *Maine* was some old ship that blew up. It has nothing to do with free speech."

Mom sits back down. "I knew that," she says. "But it's the principle. *You* might want to wear a uniform, but what if Josh next door doesn't? Why should the government tell him he has to? The government's got better things to do. Besides, I don't want to spend school board meetings arguing about solids and plaids."

She has a point.

"But what if she beats you?" I ask. "What if you're not on the school board anymore?"

"Sheila Gale won't beat me," Mom says. "I'm right about this uniform thing. Plus, I'm campaigning hard. Plus, I've got a handsome kid. Want to go door-to-door with me? Just for an hour? I haven't hit the houses on Baltimore Drive yet."

Phooey. I should have seen that coming.

"After your homework's done, I mean. What do you say?" she asks.

I sigh. "Okay." Even though I kind of like uniforms, I do want my mom to win. She's been on the school board four years, and she's good at it. She always does her homework, which means reading stacks of paper about laws and money and teaching. At the meetings, she's polite to the people who come and talk, even if they yell and curse, which they sometimes do.

While I finish my snack, Mom quizzes me on spelling words and gives me some multiplication problems to do in my head. Then she tells me she has to study up on "a personnel matter," whatever that means, and I should do my homework. "We'll rendezvous at sixteen-hundred hours. Put on a shirt with buttons.

Roger wilco?" Sometimes she talks army-radio like Dad.

"Roger wilco," I answer. "Over and out."

The first time Mom asked me to go door-to-door with her, I was all excited. I thought it would be like trick-or-treating—the people all friendly and giving you stuff.

But I was for-crying-out-loud-dumb. It turns out hardly anybody's friendly, and nobody gives you a thing. Sometimes people shut the door in your face. Sometimes you see somebody peeking out a window, but the person never answers. More people than you'd think are wearing pajamas, even if it's afternoon. One time Mom told me about this lady who was in her underwear.

At the first three houses on Baltimore Drive, nobody's home. So Mom leaves fancy letters that tell what a great and brilliant school board member she is and how it's un-American to make kids wear uniforms.

At the fourth house a little girl answers.

Mom smiles at her. "Is your mother or father at home?"

The little girl nods.

"May I speak to them?"

The little girl nods again but doesn't move.

"Uh . . . Perhaps you could ask whoever's home to come to the door?"

The little girl still doesn't move, but she yells like she's been saving her voice for this exact moment: *"Mo-o-o-o-m!"*

"Whatsamatter now, ya little— *Oh!*" A woman with messy hair and red lipstick comes down the stairs and stops when she sees us at the door. "What do *you* want?"

Mom gives her the speech: "Sorry to bother you, ma'am. I'm Teresa Plum, and I'm running to keep my seat on the Marshall City School Board." Mom holds out her hand automatically, the same way Mrs. Gale did in our class today. Instead of shaking hands, the woman pulls the little girl toward her.

Mom is used to this. She turns the handshake into a sort of a half wave and goes right on talking. "I can see you have children of your own—just as I do."

This is my big moment. Mom puts her

hand on my shoulder, and I smile and look smart. That's it. My entire job.

Then Mom continues, "And I'm sure you're vitally interested in their futures, just as I am. I hope I can count on you to pick a Plum for school board on election day?"

"Election day?" the woman repeats. "I thought you were gonna sell me God or vacuum cleaners or something."

Mom is used to this, too. She starts over. This time the lady gets it, and when we leave she takes a fancy letter and even shakes Mom's hand.

As we walk toward the next house, Mom gives me a high five. "Score one for the forces of truth and justice," she says.

We get three more nobody-homes and an old lady who smiles at me but refuses to open the door more than a crack. It's a short street so we're almost done when we get to a big house where the doorknob is shiny gold. A man wearing a business suit answers.

"Teresa Plum, eh?" he says after Mom finishes the speech. "I understand you're a member of several questionable organizations."

Most people are like the lady with the messy hair—surprised to hear there's an election coming. Some people are surprised there's such a thing as a school board. But every once in a while there's somebody like this, who knows all about it and wants to argue. I help Mom out by trying to look thoughtful.

"May I ask to which organizations you refer?" Mom says.

"AACP, NCLU . . . I can't remember all the letters just now," the man answers. "But my understanding, on good authority, is that some of your beliefs pose a threat to our impressionable young people."

"It's difficult to respond to your concerns when I don't know more precisely what they are," Mom says. "But I don't believe my lifetime membership in the Girl Scouts threatens very many young people."

This makes the man laugh, and he explains that he heard Sheila Gale speak a few days ago, and she's the "good authority" he's quoting.

"I'm sure Mrs. Gale is sincere in her commitment to our young people," Mom says. "I hope she recognizes that I am just as sincere."

The man takes the fancy letter and smiles when he says good-bye. As soon as we're back on the sidewalk, I let Mom have it: "You should've told that guy it was all a buncha lies, Mom. You're too nice!"

Mom is insulted. "I am *not* nice! But I'm not going to lower myself to the level of . . . well . . . *some people*." She opens the car door for me. "I'd rather lose," she says.

CHapter Five

On the way home, we pick up a pizza. We always get an extra large, half double-sausage and double-pepperoni for Dad, half artichoke hearts for Mom. I don't care which half I eat because I pick off the junk on top anyway.

Dad says meat puts hair on your chest, and as I carry the pizza box into the dining room, I wonder if Mom doesn't need some. Not hair on her chest—*meat*. Maybe if she ate sausage and pepperoni she'd stand up to Sheila Gale.

At 6:25, I hear the garage door squeak. When he's out of the car, Dad will take the bottle of window spray he keeps on a shelf in the garage and clean the windshield. Then he'll lock the doors, kick the tires to make sure the pressure's good, turn off the garage light and, at precisely 6:30—1830 army time—he'll walk through the kitchen door.

"Hello, troops. What's for mess?" He's right on schedule.

"Pizza." Mom kisses him on the cheek.

"Been cooking all day, huh?"

"I'm sorry," Mom says. "It's the darned campaigning, and I had to study up on personnel in case we let a certain employee go."

"I'm kidding, Teresa," Dad says. "Somebody's got to fight the good fight for education."

A couple of minutes later, we're all sitting down, and I ask Mom, "Who do you have to let go?" Suddenly I get a happy inspiration. "Is it Mr. Ditzwinkle?"

"Goodness, no!" says Mom. "Where did you get an idea like that?"

"I don't know," I mumble through a mouthful. "I just thought maybe because he's so *different* or something."

"Can't fire somebody for being different," says Dad. "It's illegal."

34

"And a good thing, too," says Mom. She looks at me. "I'll probably be able to tell you after the board meeting tomorrow night, Dex. It's called a personnel matter, which means it has to do with people's jobs. It's not fair to tell somebody else before you tell the person whose job you're talking about."

"But why would you fire somebody?" I ask. "I mean, if being different isn't a good enough reason."

"Only if they're not doing their job," Dad says. "Or if they steal money or something."

I'm usually good at puzzles and mysteries. So I crunch a bite of crust, my favorite part, and think. The school board is in charge of ten schools in Marshall City, so the person getting fired might not be anybody I know. Still . . . is there anybody working at my school who might be a criminal? Not too likely. So I try to think of somebody who isn't doing their job.

"Got it!" I say.

Mom and Dad have been talking about something else. "Got what?" Mom asks.

"It's Mr. Flumbo, isn't it? The custodian?"

Mom looks startled. "How did you—" she says. "I mean—"

I can tell I'm right. "It was easy, Mom. The rest rooms at school are *disgusting*! Every kid knows it. You wouldn't go in there even if you were gonna *explode* . . ."

"Dexter, we're eating dinner," Dad says.

"Sorry. Anyway, so Mr. Flumbo doesn't do his job. You're firing him." Mom doesn't say anything. "It's okay. You don't have to tell me. I can keep a secret, too, you know."

After dinner, Dad and I do the dishes. We call it KP—kitchen patrol—like they do in the army. Dad spent four years in the army. Mom says sometimes she thinks he never left.

After dinner, I finish one of the library books I brought home this week. Then I do twenty-five push-ups and twenty-five sit-ups and go to bed.

Life, says my dad, should be well-ordered. And mine would be. If it weren't for Mr. Ditzwinkle.

The next day is Tuesday. My briefcase is extra heavy because it's library day. I have five books to return. Most kids can take home only two books. But Mrs. Folio, the librarian, lets me take more. I am reliable, she says. I forgot Mrs. Folio when I was making my list yesterday. She likes me. That makes eight.

As I walk toward Room 29, I notice a clump of girls in the corridor. Tiffany T-1 and Tiffany T-2 are there, and Justine, and Amber, and Paula. What are they laughing at anyway? Maybe Zeke's elephant space-alien portrait.

Justine sees me first. It's not hard to be fair about Justine. She can do ten push-ups, never wears dresses, and is as good a speller as I am. Now she claps her hand over her mouth and ducks into the room. Strange.

Then Amber looks up, sees me and elbows Tiffany T-2. Paula squeals something I don't catch. Amber tries to shush her, but she's laughing too hard. So Paula says it louder. "Good morning, *blockhead*!"

Now I see what they were looking at. It's my picture. Portrait of a blockhead.

Amber stops laughing soonest, and her forehead gets this sort of "uh-oh" wrinkle. I don't look at them as I walk by. I don't hear them whisper "blockhead," and "thinks he's so perfect," and "dweebacious briefcase."

At my desk, I put my head down. I inhale and my breath stutters, same as it does after I skin my knee. I hear more people shuffling in. I squeeze my eyes shut, like that will make them all go away.

When I drew a square face, I didn't think about it looking like a blockhead. I just wanted my picture to have nice straight lines. I'm not creative. Why do I have to be? I hate art. I hate the universe. I hate Mr. Ditzwinkle.

"Hey, Dex? Y'okay?" Josh shakes my shoulder. "Y'need to go to the nurse?"

I take a deep breath. This one doesn't stutter, but when I answer, my voice sounds small. "I'm okay."

"Then you should check out the Ditz-man's jacket," Josh says.

Mr. Ditzwinkle is coming through the door, with Tiffany T-1 trotting alongside. "Oooooh, it's just beee*yoo*tiful!" She practically slobbers on his new black bomber jacket. One ninety-nine ninety-five, I remember. That raggedy orange jacket must have disintegrated.

"Thank you, Tiffany," Mr. Ditzwinkle answers. "Go ahead and take your seat now."

I feel better as the day goes on. We do math early, and there isn't any nonsense about jelly beans. Just good old word problems. Then Mr. Ditz says it's time for spelling, and there's a big moan and grumble. Before any paper airplanes take off, though, his eyebrows crawl north. Next thing, he's blowing up long skinny balloons.

"All right, class," he says, "pick an animal, any animal."

"Cat! Kitty cat!" the girls holler.

"T. rex!" yell the boys. "Pit bull!"

Justine says, "Llama!"

Tommy Finch says, "Duck-billed platypus!"

I don't say anything.

Now Mr. Ditz is twisting the balloons so they scratch against each other and squeak.

His fingers move so quickly it's impossible to see what he's doing until—"Ta-da!" He holds up a wad of tangled balloons.

The class is silent until Tiffany T-1 says, "It's lovely, Mr. Ditzwinkle. But what is it?"

The eyebrows sink behind the crooked glasses. "Well, here's the head, and . . . here's the tail, and . . ." Now he smiles. "Well, I'd say it's a duck-billed T. rex."

"No, it's not! It's a Dexter Plum!" That's Paula, of course. "See? It's got a blockhead—just like Dexter." Giggles go off like a string of firecrackers.

Mr. Ditz looks confused for about half a second. Then it's like I see the light bulb flash in his brain and—I'll never forgive him, ever—he smiles. Not his regular half smile, either. A whole, entire, lotsa-teeth smile.

"Class!" He raises his voice and straightens out his mouth. "All right, enough. It's a duck-billed T. rex, and that's final. Now let's get down with some education! Get out your spelling books."

Most people, if they feel like I do now, go

home with a stomachache. Not me. I would never let those girls think they beat me. I'm going to show them. And before I even know *what* I'm going to show them, I'm out of my seat and heading for the door.

"Dexter?" Mr. Ditzwinkle's voice sounds far away.

Only when I see the portraits in the corridor do I realize what I'm about to do. Paula's has hair made out of black pipe cleaners. A whole headful of snakes. Tiffany T-2 finished only half her heart. Justine used glitter for her blue eyes.

I hear Mr. Ditz clomping toward me. I gotta act fast. When I yank on the paper, the thumbtack shoots to the floor. *Rrrrr-ipp*. Now there are two blockheads. *Rrrrr-ipp*. There are four. *Rrrrrr-ipp, rrrrrr-ipp:* eight, sixteen . . .

"Dexter *Plum!*"

"There!" I throw the pieces, and they flutter around him like confetti.

For a second we stare at each other. Mr. Ditzwinkle's mouth is open. He must be as surprised as I am.

CHAPTER SIX

I see that same wide-mouthed look on Mom's face half an hour later. We're sitting in the principal's office.

"I don't know what got into him, Jack." She's staring at me but talking to the principal. They know each other from school board. "Dexter has always been, well . . . perfect."

Mr. Broomhockey pops open the tin he keeps on his desk. "Animal cookie?" he says to Mom.

She shakes her head. He takes a pink-frosted hippo for himself and opens the folder that's in front of him. "Looks like Dexter and Martha Dinsmore got on fine," he says. "Well, son, you're awfully quiet. What have you got to say for yourself?"

"They called me a blockhead."

"What is it? Speak up."

"They called me a *blockhead*."

"A blockhead? Why would they call you that?"

I sigh. Today has been the worst day in my life. While I waited for Mom, I had to sit on an orange plastic chair in the Morf's office. Mr. Flumbo came in—he was chewing on a lollipop like always—and I had to look away because of what I knew about his job. Then two second-grade girls came in asking for glue, and they stared at me like I was a criminal. I tried to make my face look mean, but my cheeks felt red and hot.

When Mom finally arrived, I wanted to hug her like some baby, and at the same time I wanted to hide. So far, she hasn't gotten mad. She just looks puzzled.

"Did it have something to do with the picture you tore up?" she asks.

I take a deep breath and explain. It takes a long time, even though I leave out about Mr. Ditz's lotsa-teeth smile. No way could I convince grown-ups how a smile proves my own teacher thinks I'm a blockhead.

Mr. Broomhockey shakes his head when I come to the part about the duck-billed T. rex. But when I finish, he turns to Mom and says, "Quite simple, really. The children were harsh. Perhaps Dexter here may be a little oversensitive?" He folds his hands over his belly.

"Well, I don't know that it's fair to say oversensitive, Jack. Would you like to be called a blockhead?"

Mr. Broomhockey laughs. "Seriously now, Teresa. We couldn't go around calling principals blockheads, could we?"

Mom doesn't answer.

"No, we could not!" Mr. Broomhockey looks hurt. "Wouldn't be respectful."

"I suppose not," Mom says. "But after four years on the school board, I can tell you there are times when it would be accurate."

"Teresa!"

"Well, not *you*, Jack," says Mom.

"Thank you," Mr. Broomhockey sniffs. Then he looks at me. "Dexter, I seem to remember disliking art projects when I was a youngster, too. I preferred math. Isn't that your favorite subject?"

I nod. Right now I would admit to bank robbery if it would get me out of here.

"So you see, we understand each other," he goes on. "Now, I didn't like art, but I never tore up an art project. Sometimes a man has to do what a man has to do, isn't that right?"

I nod again.

"So," Mr. Broomhockey says, "with your mother's permission, here's what I propose. First, apologize to Mr. Ditzwinkle for the disruption. Next, make yourself a nice new self-portrait. There's no need to talk detention, so long as you fulfill your part of the bargain. Do we have a deal, Dexter?"

I nod.

"Uh, Dexter, I'd like to *hear* you agree to the deal."

Mom looks at me.

"Yes, Mr. Broomhockey," I say. "Sure thing, Mr. Broomhockey. Roger wilco, Mr. Broomhockey."

"I think he agrees," says Mom.

"Seems like it." Mr. Broomhockey smiles. "Uh, Teresa, before you go, could I speak to you about that other matter?"

That must be Mr. Flumbo's job. "May I leave?" My hand is on the doorknob.

"Just let me have a word with my wayward son," Mom tells him.

Out in the corridor, Mom looks at me and tilts her head the way a dog does when it hears a strange noise. "I hope this isn't the beginning of a trend, Dexter," she says.

Shredding the picture drained the mad out of me. But now that I'm out of the principal's office, the stubborn comes back. I look down at my feet. "So what if it is?"

I hear Mom take a breath. Then she's quiet just long enough for me to feel bad. Finally she surprises me. "I love you, Dexter. Roger?"

I glance up, catch her eye, look back down. "Yeah, okay. Roger."

It would be uncool actually to hug me at school, so she gives me a half wave like when somebody won't shake hands. "I'll see you at home," she says.

On my way back to my room, I pass Mrs. Dinsmore in the corridor.

"Dexter Plum!" She smiles at me. "I miss you this year! Are you getting along well in fourth grade?"

"No," I say. "I hate fourth grade."

Now it's her turn to look surprised. "Why, Dexter. . . . I don't know what to say. You were always so *perfect* in my room."

I am getting a little tired of people calling me perfect. So I just shrug.

"Perhaps you're having a bad day," she says. "We're all entitled to those. But bad days do pass, Dexter. As the poet says, 'Even the weariest river winds somewhere safe to sea.'"

Outside Room 29, I stop and look at the empty place on the wall where my portrait used to be. I don't want to go back in there. I've had enough being stared at.

But when I hear footsteps coming, I push myself through the door. Mr. Ditzwinkle is sitting at his desk. "Welcome back," he says. "The class is reading about electricity. There are questions on page 21."

Somebody whispers something as I walk by. I hear a muffled giggle. But then Josh gives me a thumbs-up. Good old Josh.

I sit down and open the science book. My eyes are on the words, but my brain doesn't recognize them. Instead I'm making a promise to myself. I'll make a new picture, like I said. But I will never apologize to Mr. Ditzwinkle.

Mrs. Dinsmore and her poet are right. The rest of the day is passing. It even seems like Mr. Ditzwinkle is trying to be nice. Right before school gets out, he asks if I want to compete in the district spelling bee. He's got the application someplace, if he can find it. He looks on his desk and in his desk and finally in his pants pockets. No application. Finally he tries the breast pocket of his new jacket.

"Ta-da!" he says and hands it to me.

I'm counting the seconds at 3:15 again when yelling starts in the corridor. What is this, a time warp, for crying out loud? In gusts Mrs. Gale, only today she's dressed in pink.

". . . second day in a row!" says Ms. Morf, following behind, and, ". . . unbelievable nerve," and, "If only Mr. Broomhockey hadn't gone to the dentist!"

Eric's eyes are shut tight. Mr. Ditzwinkle is perched on the corner of his desk, arms folded. He reminds me of a boxer in his corner. "Yes?" he says.

The bell beeps. But Sheila Gale is louder. Right in front of the Morf and the whole class and Eric and everyone, she says, "I've had about *all* I can take, and I *think* I speak for the rest of the PC membership as well! Have you *stolen* our money, Mr. Ditzwinkle? Is that it?"

Chapter Seven

"Then what happened?" Mom asks.

It's 5:30 the same afternoon, and Mom and I are eating an early dinner so she can get to the school board meeting. Dad's not home yet.

"I don't know because he told us to 'adios and hasta la pasta.'" I squeeze a straight line of mustard on my hot dog. "Do you think he really did take the money?" I have a happy thought. "Hey! That would make him a criminal, and then you'd have to fire him, too. Like Mr. Flumbo."

"Dexter!" Mom shakes her head. "I don't know what's gotten into you lately."

Since I came home, Mom hasn't said much about the principal's office. She asked for the daily report—still three and two—then she wanted to know did I do the picture again. I told her I didn't have time. I'm glad for once she has a meeting tonight because maybe Dad doesn't have to know what happened in school today—at least not yet.

"I doubt very much Mr. Ditzwinkle's a criminal," Mom says after a minute. "But tell me, Dexter. Why don't the two of you get along?"

"That's easy," I answer. "He's crazy."

"That's an inappropriate word for a teacher," she says.

"It's not me that's 'inappropriate,'" I say. "It's *him*."

Mom chases a couple of baked beans around her plate with her fork. "What makes you say so?"

While she eats, I tell her. I think she's listening real serious, but when I mention balloon animals, she laughs.

"Mom! It's not funny! That's not how teachers are supposed to *be*! It's . . ." I have to look for the right word. "It's *embarrassing*!"

I can see Mom's trying to control herself. But two giggles escape. Finally she tells me she wouldn't want me to be a hypocrite, but I should watch the way I talk about teachers.

"What's a hypocrite?" I ask.

"It means two-faced," she says; "thinking one thing but saying the opposite."

"Two-faced." I chew my last bite of hot dog. "So you mean I don't have to pretend like I like Mr. Ditzwinkle?"

"I *mean* . . ." Mom pauses. "I *mean* mind your manners. With Mr. Ditzwinkle and every-place else. Also—finish your milk. I have to get going."

Was that supposed to be helpful? I used to think my mom was perfect. But now I wonder if she's concentrating all that hard on being a mom. Maybe she's thinking about firing Mr. Flumbo. Or beating archenemy Mrs. Gale. Maybe the only reason she's not really mad at me about today is that she's not paying attention.

Later, I'm doing my last sit-up when Dad comes into my room.

"Still doing twenty-five?" he asks. I nod, and he says, "You might think about upping it to fifty. You want to keep challenging yourself."

"Roger wilco, Dad." But fifty sit-ups sounds like a lot.

Dad sits down on the corner of my bed, and I get a bad feeling. Sure enough, he says, "What's this about Mr. Broomhockey's office?"

"How did you know?" I say.

"Don't answer a question with a question, young man."

"Sorry."

"Your mother called me at work."

So she isn't totally distracted. I lean back on my hands, ready to explain the whole thing again, but Dad stops me. "I know the gory details," he says. "What I don't know is, *why* did you do it?"

I know better than to make up excuses. I tell him the truth: I don't know. I just lost my temper.

"What was it they called you? A blockhead?"

I look at my knees. I've heard this word enough already. When I look up, I see my dad's eyes are sad. "You know, Dex," he says, "there's something I never told you before. When I was a little older than—" He stops. Downstairs, there's the squeak that means the garage door is opening. "Your mother," he says.

"Yeah. I wonder if they fired Mr. Flumbo."

He stands up. "Better go see." It's like he forgot he was going to tell me something. "You know what they say in the army, Dexter?"

In fact, I do.

"They say, 'When the going gets tough, the tough get going.' Now, what do you suppose that means?"

"Tough it out?"

He nods. "Tough it out—and don't let it happen again."

"I won't, Dad." I pull back the blankets, thinking: I do solemnly swear I will never again throw self-portrait confetti at Mr. Ditzwinkle.

CHapter Eight

A week later, all sorts of stuff has happened. Mr. Flumbo is history. Mr. Ditzwinkle still can't find the PC money. And Mrs. Dinsmore says somebody stole the jar of peppermints she keeps on her desk.

Does Prospect Avenue Elementary have a thief?

Mom said she felt bad about Mr. Flumbo because he has a family, but we kids deserve a tidy school. Now there's a new custodian named Ms. Pulita. She came around to all the rooms to introduce herself on Monday. Her keys jingle when she walks, and her face is very smiley. Now the bathrooms are clean, and I never see her sitting in her office reading a magazine and chewing on a lollipop like I used to see Mr. Flumbo.

Meanwhile, Mr. Ditzwinkle says he's still looking for the money. Lots of stories are going around: Mr. Ditz is going to get fired. He's going to get arrested. He's a professional thief, and he stole Mrs. Dinsmore's peppermints, too.

But what would he want with a whole jar of peppermints? His breath isn't even that bad.

Anyway, if I were him, I'd be scared, but so far he is acting exactly as embarrassing as usual. Today when people started a big moan and grumble, he pulled a kazoo out of his pocket and played "The Battle Hymn of the Republic." Everybody sang along the rotten-tangerine way—even me.

It was yesterday at lunch that Tiffany T-1 got her brainstorm. She said we should have a rally to show we're behind Mr. Ditz. Amber thought it was a good idea. Then Paula said, "Truly-for-sure." The rally's tomorrow, and today almost everybody in Room 29's going over to Josh's house to make signs.

I'm walking home now, real slow, because I can't decide if I'm going to help with the signs. I don't like Mr. Ditzwinkle, but practically everybody's going to be there. I've been thinking a lot about that word Mom used—*hypocrite*. She said it means "two-faced." Am I two-faced if I go?

But I'm tired of being the official fourth-grade weirdo. Sometimes I don't want to be perfect. Sometimes I want to be like everybody else.

Uh-oh. Two blocks from home, I see a new yard sign. SHEILA GALE FOR SCHOOL BOARD. That makes it three and three. Mom won't be happy with the new report.

Now I'm half a block from Josh's house. As I get closer, I can see the garage door's open, and a bunch of kids are inside.

"Hey, Dexter!" Oh no. Paula's spotted me. "Are ya coming to help? Or *not*?"

"I dunno," I say. "Maybe." And I scoot home before she has a chance to call me a truly-for-sure blockhead.

When I get to the front door and try to twist the knob, it doesn't. A couple seconds go by before I realize it's locked. "Mom?" There's no answer. So I go through the gate by the garage and around to the back, yelling, *"Hey, Mom?"* When I try the knob on the back door, it's locked, too. For one second, this weird, cold, terrible feeling hits me: I'm forgotten; nobody cares about me.

Then I get a grip. Mom probably had a meeting, and it went too long. She's been distracted lately. But she's still Mom. I can trust her. Soon she'll be back—and then I'll go over to Josh's. I'm gonna see what it's like not to be weird.

About a minute later the garage door squeaks. I run back around to the front, my briefcase banging against my leg.

"I'm *sorry*, honey." Mom is climbing out of the car. "The lines at the grocery store were long. . . ." She opens the trunk to get the groceries. "Then I bumped into this man who wanted to talk about school uniforms. . . ."

She hands me two bags of groceries, and I take them into the kitchen and set them on the counter. "It's okay," I say. "I have to go over to Josh's house anyway. I have to help make signs."

I expect her to ask, "What signs?" But she doesn't.

"What's the report?" she says, and she frowns when I tell her. "I guess I'd better write a doozy of a speech for the Veterans of Domestic Wars. Would it be too much if I brought up the Battle of the Bulge?"

"Mo-o-o-om . . ."

"I guess you're right." She hands me some gingersnaps. "See you later."

Most of the class is crowded into the garage, except for Eric of course. And I don't see Amber or Tommy Finch anyplace. Zeke hands me a paintbrush. All of a sudden, this reminds me way too much of an art project. "I don't have to be creative, do I?"

"Just paint what Tiffany T-1 tells ya to," Zeke says.

I am not crazy about having the major kiss-up tell me what to do. But I decided I'm not going to be weird. And now I've got to go through with it.

Tiffany gives me the job of painting PC NO! DITZWINKLE YES! on a sign board. Marlee Ann has already penciled in the letters. Justine is making a sign that says, OUR TEACHER'S NOT A THIEF! Tiffany T-1's reads, WE LOVE YOU, MR. DITZWINKLE! There are pink heart stickers all around the edge of that one.

Josh's job is to staple the finished signs to stakes so we can carry them at the rally.

"Can I hold the stapler for you?" Tiffany T-2 tosses her hair and blinks four times fast.

"I can do it," Josh says.

"But I don't mind. *Really*." Blink-blink-blink-blink.

Tommy Finch comes up the driveway, looking right and left. I guess he's checking to see if any kickballs are aimed at him. Josh tosses him the stapler and tries to escape into the house, but Tiffany tags right after. I hope Josh doesn't have to go to the bathroom.

I paint each letter carefully, trying hard to stay in Marlee Ann's lines so she won't get all fussy. I sure wish Mr. Ditzwinkle had a shorter name. This takes for-crying-out-loud-ever.

Finally I'm finishing the last *s* when Josh comes back with two bags of potato chips. Tiffany's carrying a pitcher of red punch, and Mr. Golden—Josh's dad—is behind them with cups.

Mr. Golden's got a big grin on his face, like having lotsa kids with paint in his garage is his idea of fun. My dad would be running around with rags and paint thinner, trying to catch every spatter.

We all drop what we're doing to go for the snacks, and Marlee Ann has a fit. "Watch it! Watch it! Keep the grease off the signs! Justine—get that punch away from there!"

"Okay, people, listen up!" Tiffany T-1 sounds like an army sergeant. We hush right up, except for crunching and slurping. "Tomorrow before school, we meet on the *dirt* by the *flagpole*! Seven-forty-five *sharp*!"

I never knew Tiffany T-1 was so good at bossing.

I'm leaning my sign against the wall to dry when Amber runs in. "My mom said it's a go!" She's all out of breath.

Only Tiffany T-1 knows what Amber's talking about. She yells and does a touchdown dance, or whatever girls do that's like a touchdown dance. "You guys, we're gonna be on *TV!*"

Tiffany squeals.

Amber nods so her curls bounce. "The news director said my mom can cover the rally. She said, 'In these troubled times, it's heartwarming for kids to show support for a beleaguered teacher.'"

"What does that mean?" Zeke asks. "What's *beleaguered?*"

Amber shrugs. She doesn't have a clue. But I ask Tommy Finch, and of course he knows. "A person or thing that's being attacked," he explains.

Amber nods. "Yeah!" Bounce-bounce-bounce.

Amber's mom is on TV, like I said. On weekdays, she sits behind a desk on the morning news on Channel 12. She talks to some man named Stan who has too much hair, and they smile and smile—unless they're talking about crime or a sick baby or something. Then they scrunch their foreheads.

Sometimes, say if a building burns down, Amber's mom goes there and stands in front of it. That's what's going to happen tomorrow, Amber explains. Only instead of a burned-down building, her mom's coming to Prospect Avenue Elementary. She'll stand there and talk, and behind her we all march in heart-warming support of our beleaguered teacher.

For crying out loud. I helped make signs. I took orders from the major kiss-up. And now I'm supposed to be on TV in front of the whole world.

When I decided not to be weird, I had no idea it would be big news.

Chapter Nine

"Hold still!" Dad orders.

We are sitting at the breakfast table, and he is combing my hair. My parents say if I'm going to be on TV this morning, I should look perfect—especially with the election so close.

"Do you really think people will vote for you because my part is straight?" I ask Mom.

"You never know." She turns a page of the newspaper. "Oh, my *heavens!*" She holds up the page. There, big as life and twice as scary, is a picture of archenemy Mrs. Gale. Underneath the picture, it says her slogan: WELL-FORMED MINDS IN UNIFORMED BODIES. Then it says: VOTE SHEILA GALE FOR SCHOOL BOARD!

Mom pushes her plate away. "It's enough to put you off your breakfast."

"Where did she get the money for an ad like that?" Dad asks.

Mom shrugs. "I can't imagine. My campaign can't even afford a new pair of walking shoes."

"Can we be done now?" I ask Dad. "It's not like I'm the star of the show. There are twenty kids with twenty signs. The most anybody'll see of me is maybe an ear."

"Then we want it to be a well-groomed ear," says Dad, still combing.

Mom asks if I want another muffin, and I say no. She says I need a good breakfast because I look "peaked." As near as I can figure, that means sleepy. I tell her that's because I *am* sleepy, but I don't tell her why. I don't tell her I kept waking up with a stomachache, and I still have one. My stomach and I are both worried about whether I'm two-faced.

Dad finally puts the comb down and pats me on the back. "There you go, son."

I stand up quick in case he gets the idea to Q-tip my ears. "Better go," I say.

"Take your raincoat," says Mom.

Outside, the sky is cloudy, and wind is rustling the tree branches. I walk fast to keep warm, and even though I get to school five minutes early, a lot of kids are already by the flagpole. I hurry to Room 29 and leave my briefcase at my desk, then I hang up my raincoat. Nobody else is wearing theirs.

When I get back outside, a purple WNUZ-12 News van is pulling up in front of the school. A skinny guy jumps out, opens the back doors, and starts hauling out equipment. Then Amber's mom gets out on the passenger's side.

"Dexter! Get over here!" Tiffany T-1 waves.

"Here—take this one." Tiffany hands me a sign. "Zeke's teaching us the words to some old song called 'We Shall Overcome.'"

I read my sign: DITZWINKLE IS THE GREATEST! It could have been worse. It could have been WE LOVE YOU, MR. DITZWINKLE! with pink hearts.

"Sound check!" says the skinny WNUZ guy.

Amber's mom holds a microphone to her mouth and says, "Good morning. This is Maggie Parks with a *heart*warming *live* report." She smiles, and her teeth are the whitest ever. "What do you think, Bob?"

"That'll do just fine," says Bob, the skinny guy.

"Okay, people!" Tiffany T-1 puts one of those cone-shaped things up to her mouth. "Amber's mom will be right over. Till then, let's practice marching. Left . . . left . . . left-right-left . . ."

I look around. Everybody in Room 29 is here—except Eric of course. "Kids? *Kids!*" Amber's mom strides toward us. "Now, the most important thing is to just *act natural*. Pretend the TV camera isn't here. Pretend *I'm* not here. Pretend there aren't tens of thousands of viewers sitting in their living rooms watching *you!*"

"When do we sing?" Zeke wants to know.

"Sing?" Amber's mom repeats. "Up to you entirely. I'm here to cover the news, not make it."

"Five minutes to air time, Maggie," Bob tells her.

We all look at Tiffany T-1. "All *right,* people," she announces. "Let's march around the flagpole singing the song Zeke taught us. Make sure parents and teachers can see us from the parking lot."

We form a circle and begin walking round and round. The kids who know the song are singing, "We shall overcome someda-a-a-ay." I hum along.

"Does the Ditz-man know about this?" Josh whispers. He's marching behind me.

"I don't think so," I say.

School starts at 8:35, and more kids are arriving. Cars on Prospect Avenue slow down when they see the TV truck. Some parents park so they can check out what's going on. There are a few people standing on the parking-lot side of us. Ms. Morf and some teachers are watching from the front doors of the building.

It feels sort of neat to have all these people looking at us. I realize I'm marching in step with Justine, who's in front of me. She looks back and smiles. I stand up straighter. My stomach feels better. I don't feel weird. I don't even feel two-faced.

Plop . . . plop—a couple raindrops splatter the dirt. I hear Marlee Ann, worrywart of the universe, say, "Oh no! What if the paint runs?" But then the sprinkles stop.

Over by the Prospect Avenue Elementary sign, Amber's mom and skinny Bob get ready for action. She's got a headset on, and she keeps tilting her head to listen. Finally she nods, turns to Tiffany T-1 and says something I can't hear. Tiffany gets a panicked look, then she gulps and looks at us. "This is *it,*" she mouths. Bob switches on a light on the video camera, and Amber's mom starts talking.

"I'm Maggie Parks with this *live* report from Prospect Avenue Elementary School." She flashes her teeth. "Here with me this morning is Tiffany Tasso, a fourth-grader in Dorian G. Ditzwinkle's class. You and your classmates are early to school this morning, aren't you, Tiffany? Briefly, can you tell our viewers what's going on?"

I swear I can feel Tiffany's heart pounding in my own chest, that's how scared she looks. But when she speaks her voice is strong: "We're here to support our teacher, Mr. Ditzwinkle. Our *beleaguered* teacher."

Amber's mom gives the camera an isn't-she-cute smile. "And why does he *need* your support, Tiffany?"

In the parking lot, a green VW bug is circling. Mr. Ditzwinkle's car. *Plop*—a drop falls on my head. *Plop-plop*—a couple more. Then I notice another car behind the Ditz-man's—a big white one. Archenemy Mrs. Gale is at the wheel.

"Some people, uh . . . *parents* . . . say he stole some money," Tiffany tells the tens of thousands of viewers sitting in their living rooms. "But he didn't do it! I know he didn't!"

Mr. Ditzwinkle parks, then hops out of the driver's seat, slams the door and walks toward the school. He's got a newspaper on his head to keep the sprinkles off. At the same time, Eric Gale flies out of the big white car like he was pushed. He's carrying his own sign and running toward the rest of us.

Amber's mom scrunches up her forehead. "So you want the world to know you believe in your teacher, Tiffany. Is that it?"

"Yes," Tiffany answers. "We *believe* in Mr. Ditzwinkle— Oh! There he is!"

Justine stops marching when Tiffany says this, and—"Oops, sorry"—I march right into her. Pretty soon the whole line has stopped, and we're all standing behind Tiffany and Amber's mom, looking at the camera and holding up our signs. Eric joins us in line and holds up his sign, so now I get a look at it.

For crying out loud! It's got nothing to do with Mr. Ditzwinkle at all! It's Mrs. Gale's giant, scary, smiling face, and it says: WELL-FORMED MINDS IN UNIFORMED BODIES! VOTE SHEILA GALE FOR SCHOOL BOARD!

"Hey—" I say. "That's not fair! She can't do that!"

But Amber's mom doesn't hear. "The man himself?" she says to Tiffany. "Let's see if we can get a *live* interview for our audience with Mr. Dorian G. Ditzwinkle, beleaguered teacher. Oh, Mr. Ditzwinkle? Mr. Ditzwinkle!"

The Ditz walks toward her. He has a crooked look on his face, even besides his broken glasses. "Hi—nice to see you. You're Amber's mom, am I right? Hi, Tiffany T-1. What's with the camera? What's the haps?"

While this is going on, I am thinking one thing: Tens of thousands of viewers are seeing Sheila Gale's campaign sign. So, trying not to mess up the line too much, I step backward and start sidestepping toward Eric's end. I don't know what I'm planning to do exactly. I can't very well tackle him right here on TV. "Sorry," I whisper. "Excuse me— *Ouch*. Sorry."

"We're here to support *you*, Mr. Ditzwinkle," Tiffany is saying. "We're here to tell the tens of thousands of viewers sitting in their living rooms right now that you *didn't steal* the PC money."

Mr. Ditzwinkle gets pop-eyed. Now that he understands the situation, I don't think he's entirely happy. But he stammers into the camera, "W-Well . . . uh, th-thanks . . . uh, of *course* I didn't steal any money."

"And there you have it, folks," says Amber's mom. "He *denies everything*! But tell me, Mr. Ditzwinkle, if you *didn't* steal the money, what happened to it?"

Mr. Ditzwinkle gulps. Maybe he didn't expect to be asked this question on live television. "Honestly, I don't know," he says after a pause. "I have a bit of an absentminded streak and—"

"What about you kids?" Amber's mom looks at us. "Does anybody have a theory about what happened to the money?"

"Maybe Tommy Finch knows!" Zeke yells.

There's a chorus of, "Yeah, Tommy Finch knows everything!"

By now we're all pretty wet. There's been a lot of rain already this fall, so the ground is getting muddy fast. Marlee Ann was right, for once: The paint on the signs is running. Amber's mom's hair has lost some of its poof.

But at least I'm making progress. There's only Paula standing between me and Eric.

"Excuse me," I whisper. Then I try to step around her, but she snarls, "Get back in line, Dexter! You're messing up our whole TV show!"

"How about it, Tommy?" Amber's mom asks, and Bob the cameraman aims the camera right at Tommy Finch's face.

Tommy Finch doesn't hesitate: "The new black jacket."

"You mean it's in the pocket?" Amber's mom asks, and Mr. Ditzwinkle reaches in to check.

"No, I don't." Tommy Finch always sounds calm and patient, like he's filled with pity that the person he's talking to is so incredibly stupid.

"*Paula,*" I hiss, "*please* just—" But Paula won't let me by. Instead she steps back and lands—*ow!*—on my foot.

"What I mean is this," says Tommy Finch. "Mr. Ditzwinkle stole the PC money, and he spent it on his new black jacket."

"Oh dear!" says Amber's mom, and *oh dear* isn't the half of it, because as I try to get my foot free, I trip and push Paula. The ground is slippery by now, and—I swear I didn't mean to do this—Paula goes right down on her rear end.

"Dexter Plum—you blockhead!" she shrieks, and then her sign slips and slaps into Zeke, and his sign slaps into Marlee Ann, and her sign slaps into Amber . . .

. . . and before you can say *hasta la pasta*, all the kids from Room 29 are shrieking and teetering and toppling into the mud.

Chapter Ten

When Paula tries to stand back up again, she slips. She's my mortal enemy, but I feel bad about knocking her down, so I reach over to help. But somebody's sign swings around and hits me in the rear . . . *SPLAT!* Now I'm in the mud, too. So much for my perfect hair—not to mention my well-groomed ears.

"*I'm* not a blockhead." I spit the mud out of my mouth so I can explain. "It's *Eric's* fault!"

"*Help!*" Paula yells. "The blockhead's *spitting* at me!" But nobody hears.

Maybe it's because mud feels so oozy and squishy. Or maybe it's because people who are covered with mud look so silly. Whatever it is, mud sure is powerful. It's like every kid who splats down into it gets instantly crazy—even me.

In no time, what started as a class of cute, heartwarming and mostly clean kids has become a free-for-all mob of TV mud warriors.

And we can't stop laughing.

"Take *that*!" Zeke heaves a handful—*splat*—right into Amber's bouncy curls.

"Oh, *yeah*?" Amber wipes her eyes and fires back, but Zeke ducks. *Splat!* The mud hits Ms. Morf, who has come running over with Mrs. Dinsmore and Mr. Wong, the P.E. teacher. Mr. Wong is running so fast he skids and comes down—*squish*—right on his white gym shorts.

Splat! Splat! Splat! The air's so full of flying mud grenades you can't tell who's throwing what. It can't be the Morf that fires back at Amber, can it? In all the mess, it's hard to know. Even Marlee Ann—usually so afraid of getting in trouble—is taking aim at Mrs. Dinsmore. Marlee never forgave her for a B-minus last year in arithmetic.

Somehow, Eric's still on his feet, his sneakers bouncing, *slurpa-slurpa-slurp*. Above the goo, his mom's face on the campaign sign flies high and clean. VOTE SHEILA GALE FOR SCHOOL BOARD!

"Pick a Plum for school board!" I shout and—I probably shouldn't do this—I grab one of Eric's slurping sneakers and yank.

Down comes Eric. Falling, he lets go of his sign and Sheila Gale's face sails into a dirty puddle. That's better.

"Hey! Amigos!" Mr. Ditzwinkle is yelling, but we're hooting and hollering so loud I can hardly hear him.

And anyway, we're not done yet. Tiffany T-1 is standing in front of us next to Amber's mom. On her face is a horrified expression, like she's witnessing—well, exactly what she *is* witnessing—a mud riot. Tiffany T-1's clean clothes, clean face, and clean hair challenge every red-blooded, ooze-caked, laughing kid from Room 29.

Tiffany T-1 is not having enough fun.

"Hey, *Tif!*" shouts Justine. *"That's* for the time you stole my eraser!" A grenade flies at Tiffany, then another and another and—*whap!*—

one misses and hits Amber's mom. Now her hair has *really* lost its poof.

But Amber's mom doesn't care. She just wipes her eyes and looks back at Bob. "You're taping now, aren't you?"

"Are you kidding?" he says, and for the first time I notice that the light is still on and the camera's still pointed at us. "It's *fabulous*! We'll be all over the network!"

All this time the rain is falling, and I suddenly realize it's cold and I'm soaked and filthy and sitting in a puddle, and what's so funny about that? I choke on my last chuckle and look around.

We seem to have drawn a crowd. The kids are laughing and pointing, but the parents don't think it's funny. And now I see something that *really* isn't funny—Mrs. Gale coming through the crowd and shaking hands as she comes. Today she's wearing pale yellow—and she's almost in range.

Is everybody thinking what I'm thinking?

"You blasted *kids*!" she yells. "There'll be an end to incidents like this once *I'm* elected. Your uniforms are going to be *spotless*! And let me say for the record—"

Splat! Whap! Sp-sp-splat! In an instant, Mrs. Gale is slimed from top to bottom. Now she's standing there dripping, her mouth open—silenced.

"Amigos!" Mr. Ditzwinkle has grabbed Tiffany T-1's megaphone. "Enough with the down and dirty!" His eyebrows are going a mile a minute. Mr. Broomhockey is jogging up behind him, and off someplace I hear the whine of a siren. It can't be the police, can it? What would the police want with us?

Skinny Bob is right about the network.

That night I hear myself yell, "Pick a Plum for school board!" and watch myself yank Eric's sneaker on both the five o'clock local news and the six o'clock national news.

By now the news guys have caught on to the fact that my mom and Mrs. Gale are running against each other. This is not the kind of thing that makes them scrunch up their foreheads. Instead, Amber's mom and Stan-with-all-the-hair can hardly keep from busting up, and the national news guy doesn't even try.

They show Mrs. Gale's face dripping mud, her mouth wide open in shock, and the guy says: "Mudslinging took on new meaning in a school board race in tiny Marshall City today . . ."

I wish somebody at my house was laughing.

Mrs. Dinsmore was the one who called the police, and something about seeing the officer in black with handcuffs dangling from his belt—well, we all laid down our squishy, oozy ammo quick. Paula even started to cry, which you wouldn't expect from Paula. So Marlee Ann gave her a hug and told her her parents would *too* still love her, which you wouldn't expect from Marlee Ann.

Ms. Morf had the smart idea of washing us all with the hose before they sent us home, and Mr. Ditzwinkle said he'd be glad to do the honors. So we all trooped over to the parking lot and, one by one, the Ditz sprayed us.

"Okay, Dexter, that's right. Tilt your head down now, and lemme do your hair. Goo-oo-ood. Spin around . . . okay. *Next!*" The water was *freezing*; my teeth chattered, and all my fingernails turned blue.

Next in line was Tommy Finch, and I'm not sure, but it seemed like the Ditz sprayed him for a very, very long time.

Then our parents had to come and pick us up. Mom made me sit on two garbage bags and a towel so I wouldn't get the seat wet, and she never said a word.

"I wish you'd yell at me," I said.

"Later," she answered. "I don't trust myself to say anything yet."

"It was the mud," I tried to explain. "There's something about mud. . . ."

"Mud," she repeated. And that was all.

Chapter Eleven

As Mrs. Dinsmore used to say, let's review:

- Two hundred PC dollars—gone
- One teacher accused of stealing it
- One custodian—fired
- One jar of peppermints—gone
- One nationally televised mud war

Isn't that enough excitement for one school year? Not at Prospect Avenue Elementary.

I'm still doing my sit-ups and push-ups, but otherwise my well-ordered life has gone to heck. Mom hasn't even been fixing my carrots and gingersnaps. She's usually out campaigning. When she's home, she's on the phone, which starts ringing before I get up and doesn't stop till after I'm in bed. If I answer it, I'm supposed to for-crying-out-loud say, "Pick a Plum for school board! Dexter speaking."

The newspaper has had stories about the mud fight and the campaign, and I'm worried Mom really might lose. Would it be my fault? But—I can't help it—I also remember how the mud made us all laugh so hard. I didn't feel weird *or* two-faced.

Today is Friday, two days after the war. My punishment is that Dad grounded me until the school carnival on Halloween.

Halloween is a week from Sunday night—two days before the school board election. I'm planning to be a Secret Service agent like I am every year. I wear the suit I have for Easter Sunday and sunglasses borrowed from Dad. I carry my briefcase. If you own a briefcase, secret agent is a real easy costume.

Dad said I'd better watch my step between now and the carnival. "If you so much as dip your toe in a puddle, you can forget about going," he told me. "Roger?"

The Halloween carnival is one of the best things all year. There's a mountain of candy, and games and prizes and everything. I for sure don't want to miss it.

"Roger wilco, sir," I answer.

Yesterday Mr. Broomhockey came into our class to tell us he was arranging an evening assembly with the chief of police, the superintendent, the school board, and all our parents. He said it was a very serious thing we'd done, that we'd stained the reputation of the school in front of the entire United States of America.

I don't think he meant to be funny when he said "stained."

Then Tommy Finch raised his hand. "Actually, it's not just the United States of America," he said. "With satellite transmission, those news broadcasts are picked up all over the world."

"*Cool!*" said Eric.

Mr. Broomhockey squinted so his eyes got tiny and black. "Thank you for another enlightening contribution, Mr. Finch."

"You're welcome, sir."

Right after that, Ms. Morf came in and pulled Mr. Broomhockey aside.

"No!" he said to her. *"But who would—"*

The Morf nodded at us and shook her head, but Mr. Broomhockey said, "It's their school, too." He turned back to us. "Ms. Morf tells me my cookies are missing. I'd suggest you students keep an eye on your lunch boxes!"

I guess the Prospect Avenue thief—if there is one—must be hungry.

And this morning we get another clue. We're standing up to say the flag salute when Mrs. Mangia, the cafeteria lady, comes over the loudspeaker with an announcement: "Teachers and students of Prospect Avenue. It is my sad duty to announce that Cafeteria Cupcake Day has been canceled. Two trays of chocolate cupcakes—with sprinkles—have vanished! A side-dish serving of tasty sauerkraut will be substituted. Thank you."

Later at the lunch table, everybody's talking about the thief.

"Who is it, Tommy Finch?" Justine asks.

"It's Mr. Ditzwinkle. Like with the PC money," says Eric. "Right?"

Tommy Finch takes a bite of sauerkraut instead of answering the question. Maybe he remembers how freezing it was when Mr. Ditz sprayed him. He chews and announces, "It's not that bad. And cabbage is full of anti-oxidants."

"I don't think we're gonna get in that much trouble, do you?" Josh asks me.

"You mean about the mud war?" I say.

Josh rips open his bag of potato chips. "There's not that much room in Mr. Broom-hockey's office, is there?"

"Not room for all of us," says Eric, who has the most experience with Mr. Broom-hockey's office. "Maybe half. You're going *for sure*, Dexter. You're in the most trouble of anybody."

There is no point in answering, so I don't. But Josh says, "Aw, lay off 'im, Eric. It was your mom's stupid poster that started it anyway."

"My mom is *not* stupid! She's gonna win the election, too." Eric sticks his tongue out at me.

"I didn't say your *mom* was stupid. I said—" Josh is arguing through a mouthful of potato chips, and Justine interrupts.

"Your mom *is* stupid," she says. "She shouldn't've yelled at the Ditz in front of everybody like she did. She's supposed to be a grown-up."

Thank you, Justine, I think. Then Tiffany T-1 chimes in. *"Yeah."*

"But what if the Ditz did it?" Marlee Ann asks. "Think how much trouble he'd get in."

"Do they send teachers to the principal's office?" Zeke asks.

Nobody knows the answer to that—except, probably, Tommy Finch. And he's not talking.

Right before school lets out, a sixth-grader comes in and hands a stack of paper to Mr. Ditzwinkle.

"Mr. Broomhockey wishes students to know he has replenished the supply in his cookie tin," Mr. Ditzwinkle reads.

We all look at each other. *"Huh?"*

So he translates: "That means he bought some more. Also," he goes on, "the assembly with the cops . . . uh . . . the *police* officers—has been scheduled for Monday night. I've got info right here for your parents to sign." The bell beeps, and he waves the papers at us. "All right, amigos! Bring these back Monday! Okie doke? Hasta la pasta!"

Chapter Twelve

Mrs. Dinsmore and her poet say every day passes eventually, but on Saturday I don't believe it. My report to Mom on Friday afternoon was bad: There were four new yard signs for Mrs. Gale and only one for her. That makes it seven to four for the archenemy, not counting us and the Goldens. So this morning Mom calls a meeting of all her volunteers in the dining room. Later, she and Dad fan out to do some more door-to-door. They don't get home till late. Dad says he's sure they rang every doorbell in Marshall City.

On Sunday morning I am so for-crying-out-loud bored I volunteer to clean the garage. That turns out to be a good idea. I scrub my palms practically raw getting two oil spots off the concrete, but now Dad and I are getting along again.

"What got into you, young man?" he asks at dinner. It's pizza. Mom is speaking to the Kill-joy Club, so we got both halves with double sausage and double pepperoni. I pick mine off and give them to Dad, so he gets quadruple meat.

"Mud," I say.

Dad nods like that makes sense. "Did I tell you about the time I got in trouble as a kid?"

I remember the other night in my room, after Mr. Broomhockey's office. "I think you started to."

"I was a puny little guy, Dexter. Not like you," he begins.

"I never knew that."

He nods. "That's why I encourage you to exercise. It's tough to be puny."

I think of puny Eric Gale. But he'd be problem child of the universe no matter *how* many push-ups he did.

"And I wore glasses, too," my dad is saying. "So one time when I was a little older than you,

I got into a dispute with this overgrown kid—a boy twice my size. I don't remember what the argument was over, but he called me four-eyes. Same as those girls called you a blockhead."

"'Four-eyes?'" I repeat. "Because you wore glasses?"

Dad nods. I am thinking *blockhead* is way worse than *four-eyes,* and I'm even going to say so. But then I see Dad's face looks pinched, like it hurts him to remember this. So instead I ask, "What did you do?"

Dad chews a bit of pizza. "Punched his lights," he says finally.

"You *did*?"

Dad nods.

"Then what?"

"Then he beat me to a pulp." My mouth must be open because he half smiles and adds, "Well, *pulp* is an exaggeration. I even landed one or two. But when it was over I was flat on the playground—and he wasn't. We both ended up in the principal's office. We got two swats each for fighting."

"You mean the big kid hit you, then the *principal* hit you?"

"Mr. Gorby," Dad says. "He had a paddle hanging on the wall behind his desk. Of course that kind of thing's against the law these days. Good school board members like your mother saw to that."

I try to imagine Mr. Broomhockey swatting anybody, but I can't. "I'm glad I live in *modern* times," I say.

"The point is, young man . . ." Dad pauses, and I think I know how I'm supposed to fill in the blank.

"Tough it out?" I say.

"Well, there's that," he says. "But there's this, too. I remember—dimly—being a kid myself. Striving for perfection is worthy. But achieving it may be something else. In the words of the philosopher, 'The perfect is sometimes the enemy of the good.'"

Wow. First there was Mrs. Dinsmore's poet; now there's Dad's philosopher. And they're both pretty good guys, it seems like. Till now, I thought I *had* to be a perfect kid—and I thought Dad had been a perfect kid.

Dad gets up and takes some foil out of a drawer. "How come you're telling me this?" I ask. "I mean, now?"

"I don't know exactly." Dad wraps up the leftover pizza, puts it in the fridge and closes the door. "I guess I never needed to before. You were always perfect."

I gnaw on my crust a minute, then ask, "So from now on, would it be okay if I was just terrific?"

Chapter Thirteen

Dad said just terrific will do, but I'm still grounded. It doesn't matter. I feel a whole lot happier. Not weird. Not two-faced. The Ditzman doesn't even seem as bad as he used to. The smartest kid in the universe said on TV that The Ditz stole two hundred dollars, and still he's toughing it out.

I'm not going to apologize, though. No way.

School on Monday is quiet. Nothing got stolen over the weekend, for one thing. And we kids in Room 29 are on our best behavior, all thinking about the assembly tonight. What are they going to do to us anyway?

Dad has to change his regular schedule so our family can eat dinner early. At 1830 hours we leave for the assembly, which is at 1900. Mom's supposed to sit on the auditorium stage. She and the other board members aren't going to say anything. They'll just be there to look like they agree with whatever the superintendent says.

There aren't very many cars in the parking lot when we arrive, but there are two TV vans.

"Oh, my heavens," says Mom.

Amber's mom and skinny Bob are standing outside the school entrance. When they see us, Bob turns on the camera, and Amber's mom talks into a microphone: "Here comes the Plum family. Teresa Plum is fighting an uphill battle for reelection to the Marshall City School Board. Perhaps you'd like to say a few words, Ms. Plum?"

Mom takes a deep breath. "This isn't live, is it, Maggie?"

The light on Bob's camera goes off. "Oh gosh, no," says Amber's mom. She sounds like a normal person when she's not talking to tens of thousands of viewers. "We're taping for the eleven o'clock. You can think a minute. Viewers can't get enough of that mud fight!"

"Oh, my heavens," Mom says again. But then she stands up straight and nods. "Okay. Let's give it a whirl."

Bob points the camera, and Mom talks to it: "My hope is that voters will stay focused on the real issues rather than allowing muddy sideshows to distract them."

"But Ms. Plum," Amber's mom says in her TV voice, "what you call a sideshow, your opponent calls 'a symptom of declining standards in our schools.'"

"Oh, hogwash." Mom's irritated now. "Our kids are getting better educations than ever. The mud incident was a simple case of youthful exuberance. Nothing a little laundry soap won't fix." She stops and Bob shuts off the camera again. "Okay?"

"A-okay!" Amber's mom grins. "You're learning to speak sound-bite real good, Teresa. You'll be running for Senate next."

More parents and kids are arriving. Mom scoots past the other TV people in the lobby, half waves good-bye to us and climbs the steps to the stage.

"But I thought Mom was mad about the mud war," I tell Dad when we've gotten seats. "I know she was mad at me."

"Of course she was mad," Dad answers. "Children over the age of four should know better than to wallow in mud. It's messy. On the other hand, it's not a case for the firing squad."

While Dad's talking, Mrs. Gale walks in. She's wearing red, white, and blue and tugging Eric with her left hand. Her right one is free to shake with any victim who gets in reach. Except for Mrs. Gale, everybody who comes into the auditorium is looking down at the linoleum, even parents. It must be having the police chief *and* the principal watching from the stage. You can't help feeling guilty, even if you never did a bad thing in your life.

I look around and see Mr. Ditzwinkle sitting with Ms. Morf. The TV people have come in, and they're standing by the back wall of the auditorium. Justine and her mom take seats in front of Dad and me. Justine looks over her shoulder and winks. I wink back, except I never can wink right, so it probably looks more like a twitch.

Then Paula and her mom sit down on the other side of my dad, and Paula leans forward and scowls at me. I ignore her. If you ask me, this is almost as much her fault as it is Eric's. She didn't have to go and step on my foot.

When everybody is finally sitting, Mr. Broomhockey says welcome and tells us we're here to "bring a sense of closure to the community regarding the unfortunate incident by the flagpole last week."

Then he introduces the chief of police. The chief starts out all friendly, but when he gets going, he lets us have it: "When youth show no regard for common courtesy, not to mention common hygiene, they can expect to reap the whirlwind they have sown!"

I think the chief's point is that somebody better punish us but good. If they don't, we'll all be in jail by the time we're twelve.

Finally the superintendent, Dr. Angela Patrona, comes to the microphone. "As superintendent," she says, "it is ultimately my responsibility, in concert with the board, to administer discipline in the event of an unfortunate instance such as the one last week. It goes without saying that we want to insure that there are no further instances of this ilk."

Justine looks over her shoulder at me, and I can tell we're wondering the same thing: How come grown-ups talk this way? Don't they remember regular words?

"In conclusion, and after due deliberation, I do hereby announce my decision," Dr. Patrona goes on. "As a result of their behavior last week, the students of Room 29 will *not* be permitted to participate in the annual Halloween Carnival on Sunday. Thank you."

The words are barely in our brains before the moan and grumble begins.

"She can't do that!" "It's not fair!" "We didn't hurt anybody!" "It's not fair!" "Everybody else gets to go to the carnival! Why not us?" "It's not fair!"

Floating above our noise is the voice of— who else?—Sheila Gale: "May I speak? Madame Superintendent? Is a *victim* allowed to speak? A *brief* comment?" She is striding toward the stage.

Dr. Patrona stammers: "Protocol doesn't—doesn't—allow for this." Mr. Broomhockey shakes his head. Ms. Morf starts down the opposite aisle like she's going to try a flanking maneuver, and Mom crosses her arms over her chest and says, *"No way!"*

"That woman moves like a Bradley tank," Dad whispers. And it's true, nothing stops her. In no time, Dr. Patrona is elbowed aside, and Mrs. Gale has the microphone.

"Let me just say," she begins, "that my supporters and I appreciate the *great wisdom* of the superintendent's decision. Even though I myself was viciously attacked by these very students, I am willing to forgive and forget—once they have taken their medicine."

The superintendent smiles and edges forward to cut her off. But Mrs. Gale isn't finished. "While we have the parents here, I'd like to add just one *teeny, tiny* thing."

Mom bounces up: "Angela Patrona, are you just going to *let* her give a campaign speech—"

Mrs. Gale's voice rises. "The *real* problem here is bigger than just one mud fight," she shouts. "The *real* problem is a school in which *discipline* has gone *out* the window! And one symptom is a certain *teacher* who sits among you voters tonight, a *known* thief! His wicked influence—"

I don't think Ms. Morf actually intended to tackle Sheila Gale. I think she just wanted to shut her up. But the effect is the same. The Morf vaults onto the stage at Mrs. Gale's feet. The Morf tries to stand up—not too gracefully, either—and bumps Mrs. Gale, who knocks into the microphone, which falls with a bonk that reverberates through the whole building. Everybody jumps, and onstage the people pop right out of their seats.

"Order! Order!" calls the superintendent. But there isn't any. Watching it, I'm thinking, If there were only some rain and some dirt we might see a grown-up replay of the great mud war.

Meanwhile, Mom is heading straight for Sheila Gale. And there's murder in her eyes.

Chapter Fourteen

Mrs. Gale sees Mom coming and skedaddles out of her way quick. Probably that's good because I don't think voters would like it if Mom strangled her worthy opponent—especially with the TV cameras whirring.

Mrs. Gale escapes down the stage steps. As soon as she gets to the audience, she starts smiling and shaking hands. I think she is glad she caused so much excitement. And for some reason, a lot of parents side with her. I can hear them as Dad and I are leaving: "She's right. What did happen to that money?" And: "My daughter says he's *unusual* for a teacher." And: ". . . shouldn't be allowed in the same room with our kids."

Mr. Ditzwinkle must be hearing it all. When Dad and I walk past, he's slumped in his seat. Mom goes over and says something to him. In the car on the way home, she tells us, "He didn't even look up, just said, 'Adios.' Poor guy. I don't think he stole anything. Do you, Dexter?"

I don't know till this second whether I think so or not. But I hear myself say, "No," and I realize I believe it. I don't like the Ditz-man, but I believe him. Besides, it makes sense that he lost the money. He's always losing stuff.

On the eleven o'clock news, WNUZ shows scenes from the mud fight while Mom's voice says, "Oh, hogwash!" Then they cut to all the grown-ups bumping into each other at the assembly. Tens of thousands of viewers in their living rooms must think Prospect Avenue Elementary has gone totally crazy.

Wednesday night, there's a school board meeting. Mom tries to talk the superintendent into changing her mind and letting us go to the carnival. But it doesn't do any good. The other board members agree with Dr. Patrona, and we still can't go.

I am proud of Mom, though. She's not quite as wimpy as she used to be. Maybe she ate some of the leftover double-meat pizza out of the fridge.

At school, the week is one big, long moan and grumble. Everybody's mad about the Halloween Carnival, and they want somebody to blame. If you ask me, it should be Sheila Gale.

But most people blame the Ditz himself. I think they're making a big mistake and listening to their parents.

At lunch Friday, Paula crumples up her paper bag and says, "You know, if he truly-for-sure stole the money, he oughta pay it back."

And Amber says, "The school superintendent called my mom's station and wanted copies of all the TV tapes."

And Josh, chewing on his peanut butter sandwich, says, "I guess he really did take it, if Tommy Finch says so."

And after that, of course Tiffany T-2 has to toss her hair and say, "I'm sure Josh is right." Blink-blink-blink-blink.

Later the Ditz writes the homework assignment on the board, and everybody's complaining. When he turns around, his eyebrows are doing the caterpillar crawl, and we all get quiet. For a second, it feels like usual.

"Ladies and gentlemen!" Mr. Ditzwinkle holds up a deck of cards. "Ordinary playing cards, right? Tiffany T-1, would you pick a card, any card?" He fans the cards. She takes one and giggles. "Show it to your classmates, Tiffany." He closes his eyes, and she holds up the queen of hearts.

"Everybody get a good look?" Mr. Ditzwinkle takes the card, puts it back with the others, and hums a circus tune while he shuffles. "Ladies and gentlemen!" he repeats. "The moment of truth! Ta-da!"

He grins and flashes the top card at us. But when he sees our confused looks, his grin melts. "Something wrong?"

"That's the ace of spades," Eric says.

"It's not my card, Mr. Ditz." Tiffany sounds heartbroken.

"Wait! Wait—my thumb slipped, that's all,"

Mr. Ditzwinkle insists. But the bell is beeping, and everybody's gathering their stuff.

Mr. Ditzwinkle sits down on his desk and watches the kids file out. I remember how Eric looked like a swatted fly that day when his mom came into Room 29. I hope I never feel as bad as the Ditz-man looks right now.

I guess I'm staring at him because he catches my eye, and it's like he wakes up. "Hang on a sec, Dex, would you?"

"Sure, Mr. Ditzwinkle." I feel so bad for him I use his whole name.

"I wasn't going to make a big deal out of this, but . . . didn't Mr. Broomhockey ask you to redo your self-portrait?"

Phooey. I wouldn't have felt bad one bit if I'd known that's what he was going to say.

"Yeah," I mumble. "He did."

"Well, how 'bout it then? You can do it at home. Due Wednesday next week?"

I nod. I wonder if he's going to ask me to apologize, too. Of course maybe I don't have to worry about any of it. I mean, by next week, Mr. Ditzwinkle could be history.

Chapter Fifteen

When I get outside, Tommy Finch is standing on the corner in front of the school. That's weird. He usually gets a ride, even though he only lives a couple of blocks from me.

"Hey, Dexter!" He sounds all excited. "I was waiting for you! We need to talk."

I wonder what the smartest kid in the universe wants to say to *me*. "Okay," I answer. "You wanna walk together?"

We start across the street, and when we get halfway, he says it: "You *must* come with me to the Halloween Carnival. It's critical."

"What?" I stop walking. "What are you talking about? You were at the assembly. We'll get expelled—"

Ho-o-o-o-onnnk—a car's horn blasts us, and I remember we're standing in the street.

"Come on, Tommy Finch," I yank his arm. "You want to get us *killed*, too? *Sorry!*" I yell to the driver who nearly mowed us down.

We step onto the curb, and Tommy Finch sighs. When he speaks again it's in his usual you're-pitifully-stupid way. "If you will come with me," he says slowly, "we can catch the Prospect Avenue Elementary School thief."

"*What?*" I stop again. But this time we're on the sidewalk, so it's safe. "I thought you were crazy when you said on TV the Ditz stole money," I say. "Now I know for sure you're crazy. How do you know who the thief is? How do you know he'll be at the carnival?"

"It could be a 'she,'" says Tommy Finch.

"So you *don't* know who it is?"

Tommy Finch shakes his head. "But I do know whoever it is will be at the carnival. Look what's been stolen so far: Mrs. Dinsmore's peppermints. The cafeteria cupcakes. Mr. Broomhockey's cookies. Do you see a pattern?"

I'm beginning to. "And there'll be a mountain of candy at the Halloween Carnival," I say.

"Precisely, Dr. Watson. What more logical target for the Sweet-Tooth Thief?"

I don't say anything while we walk past the thrift store, All Sortsa Sports and Hobby Lobby. Something's bugging me, and I'm trying to think what it is. Suddenly I know: "But what about the money? The PC membership money?"

"It's a sticking point," Tommy Finch admits. "But perhaps the thief purchased candy with it."

"Not a black bomber jacket?"

Tommy Finch turns red. "I feel just terrible about that," he says. "That's one reason I want to catch the real thief. I want to help Mr. Ditzwinkle because what's happened is partially my fault."

"But for all you know Mr. Ditzwinkle *is* the thief," I say, even though I don't really believe it. "Did you think of that?"

"Of course I thought of it," Tommy Finch answers. "I think of everything. But he can't be. Remember the jelly beans we had for math? He didn't eat a single one."

We turn the corner by Gentleman's Closet, and I start looking for yard signs. Of course I know there are holes in Tommy Finch's theory. And he must know it, too. Still, I have to admit the theory makes sense. Tommy Finch may have been wrong once, but he's still Tommy Finch. If he's right, maybe we really could catch the thief.

I wouldn't mind being a hero. "But why are you asking me?" I ask. "I don't even like Mr. Ditzwinkle."

"Three reasons," he says. "First, you're the second smartest kid in Room 29. Second, your mom is running against Mrs. Gale, so I know you don't like *her*. Third, I'm scared to do this by myself. We're talking about a criminal, after all. Catching him—or her—might be dangerous."

I look down the block to my left, and there's another yard sign for Mrs. Gale. *Phooey*. I'm not even going to tell Mom about this one. "Okay," I say to Tommy Finch. "I'll do it." It would help Mom's campaign if her son turned out to be a hero two days before the election, right?

I try not to think about the other possibility: what it would do to her campaign if, two days before the election, her son got thrown out of school.

Chapter Sixteen

Tommy Finch and I meet at the thrift shop Saturday morning when it opens. We don't have much money, so that seems like a good place to get costume stuff. To get away with this, we'll need brilliant costumes. I wish I had a brilliant idea.

I'm poking around in the blanket section, wondering if I could dress up as a Navajo ghost or something, when Justine comes through the door by the cash register.

"Hey, Dexter! Tommy Finch!" she says. "Are you looking for Halloween costumes, too? I always get stuff here. It's so *funky*."

Tommy Finch and I look at each other like we've been caught red-handed.

"Yeah. We're getting Halloween costumes," I say at the exact moment that Tommy Finch says, "No, we aren't shopping for costumes."

Justine laughs. "Okay. What's the big secret?"

"Maybe she could help us," I say to Tommy Finch.

"Maybe." Tommy Finch sounds reluctant.

"I bet she has good costume ideas," I say.

"Loose lips sink ships," Tommy Finch says. Ships? Lips? What is he talking about now?

"If they torture her, she might tell," he explains s-l-o-w-l-y.

"Torture?" Justine's eyes light up. "This is getting *interesting*."

Tommy Finch tilts his head and looks at Justine again. "Okay, Dexter," he says finally, "you can tell her."

I tell Justine about Tommy Finch's theory and our plan. I'm about to explain the costume problem, but she's too quick. "So we need costumes that hide us good? That's easy."

"Wait a minute. What do you mean 'we'?" I want to know.

"You think you're sneaking into the Halloween Carnival without me? No way." Before I can argue, Justine is telling us her idea. At first, Tommy Finch and I say forget it, but the more she talks, the more we have to admit she makes sense. And anyway, you can't be embarrassed when nobody knows it's you.

"You know what, Dexter?" Tommy Finch says. "I might've been wrong about your being the second smartest kid in Room 29. You're only the second smartest *boy*."

We're heading toward the cash register with our stuff when I notice something bright orange on one of the clothes racks. It's a second before I realize what it reminds me of.

"Hey—isn't that Mr. Ditz's old orange jacket?" I ask.

Justine grabs it off the hanger. *"Perfect!"* she says. "The finishing touch for your costume, Dexter."

I take it by the collar like maybe it has cooties or something. "Wear *this*?" I say.

"Dexter," says Justine, "trust me."

Chapter Seventeen

Sunday afternoon I have to lie to my parents about where I'm going. I am not good at lying, even for a good cause like now. And I know my parents are surprised when I say I'm going to Tommy Finch's house for dinner, just like his parents must be surprised when he says he's coming to my house. It's not as if we're friends or anything.

We meet at Justine's to put on our costumes. *Her* parents think we're going trick-or-treating. One trouble with lying is it's tough to keep track of who you tell what—or, as Tommy Finch would say, *whom* you tell what.

Yesterday at the thrift store, Justine told us not to worry about masks because she had some at home. Now we're in her room getting dressed, and she hands me mine. "No way!" I say when I see what it is. It's bad enough I'm dressed up as what Justine calls an exotic princess—scarves tied over my head and around my neck, bracelets, necklaces, and two layers of lotsa-color skirts—but I will *not* wear a Cinderella mask, too.

"I'm sorry," Justine says. "It's left over from when my sister was our age. But you could wear this one if it's better." She holds up Bambi.

I don't say anything; I just grab Cinderella.

"Remember," Justine says. "The best part is nobody will believe it's you if you're dressed as a girl. It's too outrageous."

"What about you, then? How come you're not dressed as a boy?"

"It's better if we match," she answers. "Everybody will wonder who those three cute girls are, and nobody will think maybe two of them are boys."

I put on the Cinderella mask and look in the mirror. "If either of you laughs, I'm punching your lights," I grump. But then I look over at

Tommy Finch—wearing scarves, bracelets, necklaces, skirts, and a Snow White mask—and I crack up. This makes him bust up, too, and pretty soon we're all three out of breath, we're laughing so hard. It's almost as good as the mud war.

"Hey—it's five to five," Tommy Finch says. "We need to leave."

"Don't forget your lovely orange jacket," Justine tells me.

I look around and spot it lying on the floor with all the extra clothes. After I put it on, I check the mirror one more time. "Do you think it goes okay?"

"Its *gorgeous*, dahling," Justine says. "And besides, it's cold out. You'll need it."

The Halloween Carnival happens on the upper playground by the cafeteria because that's where the lights are. There are about twenty booths with games and food, and at the end there's a costume parade. They give candy prizes for the best costumes and divide what's left for trick-or-treat bags.

It takes forever to walk to school. My legs keep getting tangled in my skirts, and I trip and pick them up and reorganize them all. I don't see how girls do it. Of course we have to wear our masks the whole time, too. We don't want anybody on their way to school to see the three cute princesses are really us. My face sweats underneath Cinderella, and my head itches under the scarves. We're finally coming through the playground gate when Justine turns to Tommy Finch and asks, "What's the plan?" Her voice is muffled under her mask so it sounds more like, "Washa pwan?"

"Plan?" says Tommy Finch.

"You know." Justine mimics Tommy's you're-too-pitifully-stupid way of explaining. "How do we catch the Sweet-Tooth Thief anyway?"

"Well," says Tommy Finch, "I guess the best way would be simply to collect the clues and investigate until we deduce who it must be. Then we nab him—or her."

"That's your plan?" Justine can't believe it. "Boy, some genius you turned out to be!"

119

We're getting closer to the booths, and three grown-ups walk toward us. Right away I panic. I feel so much like me, even under all this stuff, I can't believe nobody else can tell. It's even worse when the grown-ups get close and I see one is Mrs. Dinsmore.

"Well, don't you three look *sweet!*" she says. "Now, let me guess. Is that Jeanne Rice under there? And you two must be Vanessa and Ginnie!"

Tommy and Justine just stand there, and I realize they're as scared as me. "How did you guess?" I answer—only because of the mask it sounds like, "Hoe didjoo gesh?"

Mrs. Dinsmore laughs. "I ought to know my own students!"

Justine tugs my arm, and we walk on. "Bye, Mrs. Dinsmore!" I call. I feel better now that we fooled somebody. Maybe this will turn out okay.

As we approach the booths, I hear spooky *whooo-ooo-ooo* sounds coming from a loudspeaker and giggles and squeals from kids playing games. There's a line for the haunted house, like there always is, and a crowd around the cotton candy booth. I count a dozen space aliens—all sizes—and the usual clowns, fairies, firefighters and witches.

I see a lot of princesses, too, but I have to hand it to Justine. We three are easily the most exotic.

Some of the older kids have truly scary masks, the rubber monster-movie kind that you pull over your head. A kid as tall as a grown-up walks by wearing one of those. It's got yellow fangs and scars and dripping blood and wrinkles—the works. The whole thing looks extra creepy because a lollipop is sticking out of the mouth.

Most of the parents and teachers working in the booths are dressed up, too. Taking hot-dog money, Mrs. Gale is wearing a white blouse, a blue skirt and knee socks. Her hair is in pigtails tied with ribbons.

"What's she supposed to be?" I ask.

"That's the uniform she wants girls to wear if she wins," Justine says. "Boys are lucky. They get to wear pants."

My exotic princess skirts are tangled around my legs again. I yank them so I can keep walking. "*Some* boys are lucky," I say.

Just then I notice Mr. Ditzwinkle taking tickets at the haunted house. I'm surprised to see him here. I figured if we kids in Room 29 couldn't come, he wouldn't, either. The Ditz has a black-and-red cape over his shoulders and vampire fangs, but with his crooked glasses, he doesn't look too scary.

"Hey, look!" I see something else. "They've got the fishing game this year. Let's play it; want to? I always win something at that one."

"Dexter!" Justine says, then she realizes what she's said and puts her hand over her mouth hole. Luckily, the mask kept anybody else from hearing, and she hisses at me, "We are here for a purpose! We can't go have *fun!*"

"I don't see why we can't have a little fun," I hiss back. "We ought to be blending in with the crowd."

"Okay. Fine," says Justine. "Genius here has failed us, and you're gonna play games. I guess *I'll* have to come up with a plan." She shakes her head. "Typical men!" Then she realizes she's done it again and slaps her hand over her mouth hole.

"Come on," I say. "We'd better get away from all these people before Miss Loose Lips announces our names on the loudspeaker."

The three of us sit at one of the lunch tables between the booths and the back of the cafeteria. The kid with the scary mask walks past, but otherwise there's nobody over here.

None of us says anything for a few minutes. I scratch my head under my scarf and my nose under my mask. It sure is uncomfortable being a princess. I wish either Justine or Tommy Finch would come up with a perfect plan. But then I remember what my dad's philosopher says— about how "perfect is the enemy of good." Can't I come up with a plain old *good* plan myself?

"They keep the candy in the cafeteria," I say. "Right?"

"The pantry, probably," says Tommy Finch.

"Yeah, that's where the powdered potatoes are," says Justine.

"So the Sweet-Tooth Thief will be in the cafeteria pantry," I say.

"But how does the thief get in?"

"Break a window?" Justine suggests.

"Shoot out the lock?" says Tommy Finch.

"I don't think so," I say. "If that was it, there would've been damage to the school before now."

"That's true," Tommy Finch says. "So that might mean—"

"—the thief has a key." I finish his sentence for him.

"So we have to think who has keys," says Justine. "There's the cafeteria ladies. Mr. Broomhockey. Ms. Morf. And . . . Uh-oh." We look through our eyeholes at each other, then we say it at the same time: "The teachers?"

I think for a minute. Have we risked getting expelled and we're only gonna catch Mr. Ditzwinkle after all? But then I remember something. "No," I say. "The teachers don't. Not to the cafeteria. Remember how when the Ditz-man's keys fall out of his pocket there aren't that many? I think the teachers only have keys to their rooms."

"You're right," says Justine.

"But wait a second," I say. "I know who has keys—heaps of keys! Ms. Pulita, the custodian. They jingle on her belt loop when she walks. She must have keys to everything."

Tommy Finch nods. I can tell he's excited. "It's logical, too," he says. "She arrived at about the same time the stealing started."

I stand up. "If we don't hurry, it'll be too late."

Tommy Finch gets to his feet, then Justine does, too. "Okay," she says, "but where are we going?"

"To the cafeteria pantry. There's a thief there, and we've gotta catch her."

"But *how?*" Justine whines.

"Justine," I say, "trust me."

Chapter Eighteen

"This is a little spooky, isn't it?" Justine asks. We're walking into the darkness away from the lights of the carnival.

I don't answer, but I'm thinking it's a *lot* spooky—especially on Halloween night. The school building creates black shadows, and any second I expect some ghoul to pop out of one and chase after us. We're getting close to the cafeteria when Tommy Finch points around the corner. "The pantry's on this side," he says. "You've been in it, Justine. Is there a window?"

"Yeah, but it's way high up."

"Could you see inside if you stood on my shoulders?" I ask.

Justine giggles. "I guess so. But what if someone sees us? We won't look like such cute little princesses then."

"Can we take our masks off now?" Tommy Finch whines. "There's nobody back here but us. Snow White is driving me crazy."

Cinderella's killing me, too. But we can't risk it. "Someone might come this way from the front of the school," I say.

We round the corner, and my heart starts to pound. It's dark and deserted over here. The sounds of the carnival are faint, but every once in a while there's a *whoo-ooo-ooo-ooo* from the loudspeaker. At least I hope it's from the loud-speaker.

"Which window is it?" Tommy Finch asks. There are five in a row along this part of the wall, all about two kids high.

"I don't know for sure," Justine says. "I never counted. Maybe— *Hey!*" She suddenly speaks in a whisper. *"Did you see that?"*

"I didn't see—" Tommy Finch starts to say, but then he does see it, and so do I. There's a light jumping around inside the second window. Somebody's in there with a flashlight.

"Get back!" I whisper, and at the same instant, I push Tommy and Justine up against the wall.

"Ow! What did ya do *that* for?"

"The thief might've seen us there, but not here. I hope she didn't look out the window already."

"Now what?" whispers Tommy Finch.

"She has to get out of the building somehow," I whisper back. "When she does, she'll be carrying the candy. That's when we nab her."

But I'm wrong. No sooner do I say it than somebody tries to nab *us*. "You kids!" Mr. Wong hollers from the direction of the carnival. "I mean *you*! Come back over here this *minute*!"

If we go, we're caught—and with no thief to make us heroes, either. So what choice do we have?

We don't even look at each other. We run for it.

Justine is fast, but Tommy Finch isn't. And my darn skirt trips me so I stumble every other step. As we run along the side of the building,

I think I hear Mr. Wong's track shoes gaining on us.

"I can't—" Tommy Finch gasps. "You guys . . . go on—"

The side door to the cafeteria is a few feet ahead of us now. There's no chance in heck it could be open, but I reach for the knob anyway. To my amazement, it turns. *"Quick, get inside!"* I tell them.

A second later, the door clicks shut and we're standing in the lunchroom of the cafeteria. There are windows in the cafeteria kitchen, but none in the lunchroom. Something to do with the thermostat, Mom told me once. Anyway, when the lights are off it's totally black. I lean against the door, breathing hard. "We'd better get outta here fast," I whisper. "I don't know how to lock it. We can't keep whoever is out there out there."

"Can't we turn on a light?" Justine asks.

"You want Mr. Wong to catch us for sure?"

"It might . . . ," Tommy Finch breathes, ". . . be preferable to having somebody *else* catch us."

That's when I remember we're not alone in here. Somewhere nearby is the Sweet-Tooth Thief.

"Let's stick together," I say, and blindly I reach out and catch hold of Tommy's and Justine's hands. We expect the door to burst open any second, so the three of us sidestep away from it—and away from the pantry. We keep our backs against the wall so we'll be harder to see from the doorway, and so we don't run into the lunch tables in the middle of the room.

The cafeteria opens into the school's main corridor. If we can get that far, we should be able to go down the stairs and out the front door. The carnival is in back, so there's a chance we'll get away.

Not a very good chance, I admit.

It's slow moving along the wall. My heart never stops pounding, and I can feel Justine's and Tommy's palms are as sweaty as mine. We're about halfway to the corridor when a noise makes the three of us freeze. Is the door finally opening? No. It came from somewhere else. Next we see a beam of light shining first on the floor, then on the clock to our right. It's the thief! She must have her loot and be on her way out, too.

Is she coming this way? What if she catches us in the beam of her flashlight?

"Get down!" Justine whispers, and at the same time she pulls my hand, so now we're crouching against the wall. I've never been so scared, but I can't help thinking how ridiculous we three exotic princesses would look if the lights came on.

From somewhere out in the lunchroom there's a thud followed by a squeak then a bump. The thief must be running into the lunch tables as she comes across the room— right toward us. *Bump.* She's getting closer. *Squeak.* Closer yet. I wonder why she turned off her flashlight? She must be aiming for the door we came in, but her sense of direction is off. If she hits the wall, she hits *us*.

I take two deep breaths to calm down. The Sweet-Tooth Thief wouldn't actually hurt anybody, would she? She eats candy, not kids, right? I remember Ms. Pulita's smiley face. It's kind, not wicked.

But at that moment, a truly wicked face appears—a horrible ghost head with yellow fangs and scars and dripping blood and wrinkles. It's about ten feet in front of us, floating in the air, and it has *no body*.

"Aaaaaaaaaah!" I don't know if it's Justine or me or Tommy Finch who screams—maybe all three of us at once. My heart feels like it's going to jump right out of my rib cage, and Justine's fingernails are gouging holes in my hand.

"Hey! Stop there!" yells a man's voice. It isn't the ghost, but I don't want to stick around and find out who it *is*.

"Run!" I shout. We let go of each other's hands and crowd and trip and topple trying to get to the main corridor. At one point I look behind us, and the ghost has vanished, but something's still in the lunchroom. I can feel it. *We've got to get away.*

Chapter Nineteen

My stupid skirt is so tangled now that I can't run for my life—I'm more like taking baby steps for my life. My shin hits a bench, I ricochet, and my elbow bashes the wall. From the bumping sounds around me, I'd say Tommy and Justine are doing about the same.

Then I hear something familiar, something I hear all the time: *Crrr-r-r-a-a-a-a-ack.* I know what it is, but my mind is so rattled it takes a second to place it. Then I do: It's the sound of glasses being stepped on. Mr. Ditzwinkle's glasses. After that there's a rapid succession of noises from right about where the ghost was. *"Ow!"*—*"Sorry, did I . . ."*—*"Oooooofff!"*

And finally one great big thud.

It's silent for a moment, but I have the feeling whatever's happened is good, that there's no danger anymore. Then—*click*—the lights come on.

"There are two things I still don't understand," Mr. Broomhockey says. "Oh—my manners! Pardon *me*." He pops open the cookie tin he keeps on his desk. "Dexter? Justine? Tommy Finch? What about you, Mr. Ditzwinkle? Please, take a cookie."

"Thank you, sir." I take a pink-frosted tiger, and I wish I could have a dozen more. There's nothing like being scared out of your skin to make you hungry.

It's half an hour later, and my heartbeat's finally back to normal. Our parents are coming to pick us up, and we're waiting in Mr. Broomhockey's office. Even though we didn't technically catch the thief ourselves, Mr. Broomhockey said our intentions were good, and we're not going to get in trouble. At least not with the school. I don't know what Mom and Dad will do to me.

When the lights came on, the Vampire Ditz-winkle was in the middle of the lunchroom with a body at his feet. Next to the body was a big plastic bag with Halloween candy spilling out of it. As I watched, the body moaned and rolled over, and I saw it was the big kid with the movie-monster, pull-on mask.

But where was Ms. Pulita? Wasn't she the Sweet-Tooth Thief?

"Who's over there?" Mr. Ditzwinkle squinted in our direction. "You kids want to give me some help? My glasses must be here some-where. And this guy might need a doctor."

Tommy Finch and Justine were right next to me. Our masks were still on; we were still in disguise. I halfway wanted to keep running. But the Ditz-man needed help, and so did whoever was on the floor. "Come on, guys." I pulled my mask off, and it felt so good I pulled the skirts off, too. I had my jeans on underneath of course, and I left the ratty orange jacket on.

Soon Mr. Ditz's crooked glasses were back on his nose, and the big kid was resting flat on one of the cafeteria tables. Justine called 911 from the cafeteria office, so the cops and an ambulance were on the way.

"Let's see who it is we've got here," said Mr. Ditzwinkle. Gently, he unrolled the rubber mask and pulled it up over the kid's neck, chin, lips, nose, eyes . . .

"Mr. Flumbo!" we all said at once. Our former custodian's eyelids fluttered, but they didn't open.

"What an idiot I've been," said Tommy Finch. "He was always eating lollipops, remember? He must have made duplicate keys when they fired him."

"Will he be okay?" Justine asked.

"Just a bump on the head, I think," Mr. Ditzwinkle answered. "But the district's not gonna like it that he stole all those sweets."

"Will he have to go to jail?"

"Probably not, Dexter. He'll have to pay for what he stole and maybe check in with the police for a while. To prove he's behaving himself."

* * *

"What don't you understand, sir?" Tommy Finch asks Mr. Broomhockey. I can tell Tommy Finch will be happy to explain anything to the principal in his usual, patient, it's-not-your-fault-you're-stupid way.

"First of all, Mr. Ditzwinkle—Dorian—how did you catch him? What were you doing in the cafeteria anyway?"

"Ms. Morf sent me in to get the candy," says Mr. Ditz. "Only I couldn't find the light switch. Then I saw this *thing* in the middle of the room, like a *monster* or a *ghost* or—"

"—a scary Halloween mask," says Tommy Finch.

"Right," says Mr. Ditzwinkle. "Mr. Flumbo must have heard the kids, and he lit up his mask from below with a flashlight to try to scare them."

"He succeeded," I say.

Mr. Ditzwinkle smiles. "Anyway, I yelled at him to stop and ran in his direction, but it was dark and I kept bumping into things. I guess

137

the last thing I bumped into was Mr. Flumbo himself. My glasses fell off, I stepped on them, and then . . . well, I'm not sure. He might've tried to hit me with the flashlight, or maybe he was only trying to point it at me. The end result was *I* got hold of it and *he* got thumped. I never meant to hit him at all."

"And then you turned the lights on," Justine says.

"And then I turned the lights on," Mr. Ditzwinkle repeats. "And I spotted one weird-lookin' princess dudette and two weird-lookin' princess dudes—one of them wearing my old orange jacket, I might add."

"Thrift shop," I say.

"Very stylish," says Mr. Ditzwinkle.

"What's the other thing you don't under-stand, Mr. Broomhockey?" Tommy Finch must be hoping he'll at least get to explain something.

"It's the same old question," Mr. Broom-hockey sighs. "What happened to the PC money? Did Mr. Flumbo steal that, too?"

No way Tommy Finch is going to touch *that* question. But I do: "I don't think Mr. Flumbo did take it, sir. The PC money disappeared before the board even fired Mr. Flumbo. I bet he stole stuff because he was mad about that."

"You're a bright boy, Dexter," says Mr. Broomhockey. "But we still don't have an answer to my question."

Mr. Ditzwinkle is looking at the floor. "Like I said on TV," he begins, "I'm afraid I lost it. I didn't pay it back because I kept thinking it would turn up. Well . . . that and because I was mad at Sheila Gale for accusing me the way she did. I didn't want to look like I was admitting anything. Especially after the assembly. I guess I'm just stubborn."

"Wouldn't you agree, Dorian," Mr. Broomhockey asks, "that the time has come for you to stop being stubborn?"

"You're right, Jack. Let me just see if I can find my checkbook somewhere." Mr. Ditzwinkle takes off his Dracula cape and fumbles in his pants pockets. Out come keys, a wallet, a taco sauce coupon, baseball cards, and vampire fangs. "No checkbook," he says.

Mr. Broomhockey folds his hands over his belly. "We'll wait."

So the Ditz tries the pockets of his jacket. Out come a kazoo, six pennies, a tiger-striped paper clip, and a tea bag. He shrugs. "No checkbook."

"Breast pocket?" says Mr. Broomhockey.

I bet it's there. That's the pocket the spelling bee application was in the day the Ditz couldn't find that.

And then I get the brainstorm.

Wouldn't it be weird if . . . I slide my hand into the breast pocket of the ratty orange jacket I'm wearing.

Something's in the pocket, all right.

"I think," I say, "that maybe I have the answer to Mr. Broomhockey's question."

Everybody watches as I pull the something out of the pocket. It's a white envelope. Crumpled. Coffee-stained. Labeled "PC."

And full of membership money.

I hold it up for them all to see. *"Ta-da!"*

Chapter Twenty

It's Wednesday morning before school, and I'm at my desk in my room, putting the finishing touches on the self-portrait I'm supposed to turn in today.

According to Maggie Parks, WNUZ News, I'm a hero. And Tommy Finch is a hero. And Justine is a hero. And the Ditz—he's *really* a hero. With our assistance, he caught the notorious Sweet-Tooth Thief, thus guaranteeing students of Prospect Avenue Elementary the right to enjoy cupcakes, cookies and candy for the foreseeable future.

Anyway, that's what Maggie Parks and Stan-with-too-much-hair said on the news Monday.

Hero is not exactly the way the parents put it.

"Things turned out well," Dad told me, "but that doesn't excuse the lie you told. Does it?"

I had to admit it didn't. I'm grounded again, and so are Justine and Tommy Finch. At least our parents let us talk on the phone. We heroes have to keep in touch.

Yesterday was the school board election. Being a hero was supposed to help Mom's campaign, right? A bunch of her volunteers came over, and we all stayed up watching the election returns on TV. At 11:00, Stan announced it. The count was close—and Mom had lost.

She kept it together while she said good-bye to everybody. But when the door closed, she started crying like her heart had broken. We all sat on the couch for a long time not talking. Finally I went up to bed. I felt awful for Mom, but a little part of me thought maybe now I'd get my carrots and gingersnaps back.

I sit back and study this self-portrait in front of me. It's a lot different than the last one. I didn't want another blockhead, so I drew circles like crazy: a big one for my head, then masses of smaller ones on top of it. I guess they must be the hair.

Then I made circle glasses and a circle body. Now I sit back and study him. He looks familiar, even though he doesn't look a thing like me. But didn't Tiffany T-2 make a valentine, for crying out loud? And Mr. Ditz told her it was creative. I can always say what she said, that this is the *real* me.

Mr. Ditzwinkle said my first portrait needed colors. So to finish this one, I put an orange crayon in the compass and draw some circles on the round body. Then I add yellow petals— daisies. There. Dexter Plum: hero and colorful guy.

As I come downstairs, I hear somebody laughing in the kitchen. Mom? What does she have to laugh about?

"Look at this, Dexter!" When I walk in, she holds up the newspaper and grins.

I see the story that says she lost. "Yeah, Mom, I know." I hope she hasn't snapped or something.

"Not *that*." Dad points. *"This."*

Below the main election story is a littler one with this headline:

D. A. Eyes School Race Irregularities
Says uniform manufacturer
paid for Gale campaign

Now I get it. "You mean that's how she had the money for those big ads?"

"That's right," says Mom.

"And that's cheating?" I ask.

"A court will decide if it's against the law," Dad explains. "But the voters will think it's cheating."

"So then you'll get to be on the school board again!" I say to Mom.

"Well," she answers, "could be. But over-night I've been thinking. . . ."

Uh-oh. *"What* have you been thinking, Mom?"

"Well, what do you think of 'Pick a Plum for Senate'?"

What do *I* think? I think this: Bye-bye, gingersnaps.

At school, Tommy Finch and Justine and Josh tell me they're sorry about my mom. But I explain about the newspaper today, and then Eric comes in, and he doesn't look quite as bouncy as you'd expect. I guess I don't mind fixing my own snacks after school. I bet senators get pretty distracted. But even if she's not the perfect mom anymore, she'll still be terrific. And terrific is good enough.

Besides, "Senator Plum" sounds cool.

Now that the Ditz-man and I are partners in crime fighting, most people figure we're pals. I am not so sure. The first thing after the flag salute, he asks me to turn in the self-portrait.

"Perhaps you'd like to share it with your classmates, Dexter," he says.

Not really, I think. But I pull it out of my briefcase and hold it up anyway. The reaction is total silence.

Phooey. I tried, didn't I? Do I have to do it over? I know I made the glasses a little crooked, but it doesn't have to be perfect, does it?

Finally, Mr. Ditzwinkle says, "My goodness."

Then Josh says, "It looks just like him!" and Tiffany T-2 squeals, "A*dor*able!" and Paula says, "What a totally-for-sure kiss-up," and Eric says, "Gag me," and Marlee Ann says, "Perfect!"

What are they talking about?

"There *are* just a coupla things, though," Mr. Ditzwinkle says. "May I?" He reaches into one pocket, then another pocket, then finally a third pocket, where he finds a black pen. Then he takes my portrait and draws two caterpillar-furry eyebrows behind the glasses.

That's when I see it. My picture's not a self-portrait one bit.

It's a portrait of Mr. Ditzwinkle.

I can't for-crying-out-loud believe it. First a blockhead, now this. I *hate* art.

"I didn't *mean* to make a picture of you," I say. "It was just that I wanted it to be circles and I got carried away and . . ."

But even while I'm talking, I know it's not totally true. Some part of me—I guess it's the part that wakes me up at night—knows that me and Mr. Ditz are alike. We're both stubborn. And we're both weird.

"I can see how that would happen, Dexter," he says. Then he tacks the portrait up under the clock. "How does it look?"

"Uh . . . Could I . . . ?" I ask.

"Be my guest."

I don't know why. But now that I've made this self-portrait of the wrong guy, I see—a little—who I am: a nine-year-old with a briefcase. Who likes black jelly beans and pizza crust. Who has a stomach that's always worrying about something—like how many push-ups to do before bed. Oh . . . and a hero.

But it's like the Ditz-man's guy Polonius said: To thine own self be true.

I think I know what that means now. Even if everybody thinks you're weird, you've gotta pay attention to the handsome guy inside.

I get up, pull the picture from the wall, flip it over and hang it upside down.

Mr. Ditzwinkle smiles at me. Not his usual half smile, but a whole, entire, lotsa-teeth smile. Maybe he still doesn't like me. But the smile he gives me is real just the same. It's the kind of smile one weird guy gives another.